I.D.
CRIMES OF IDENTITY

I.D.
CRIMES OF
IDENTITY
The Official CWA Anthology

Edited by Martin Edwards

British Library Cataloguing in Publication Data available

This Large Print edition published by BBC Audiobooks Ltd, Bath, 2007.
Published by arrangement with Comma Press

U.K. Hardcover ISBN 978 1 405 64118 0
U.K. Softcover ISBN 978 1 405 64119 7

Printed and bound in Great Britain by
Antony Rowe Ltd., Chippenham, Wiltshire

Contents

Introduction

*Who*dunit? Puzzles of identity lie at the heart of much of the best crime fiction. Think of such diverse and marvellous books as Conan Doyle's *The Hound of the Baskervilles*, Josephine Tey's *Brat Farrar*, Walter Mosley's *Devil in a Blue Dress*, Ruth Rendell's *A Sleeping Life* and Raymond Chandler's *The Long Goodbye* and you will see what I mean. Impersonation and disguise have featured in mystery stories so often that, as long ago as the 1920s, novelists and commentators such as Ronald Knox in the UK and S.S. Van Dine on the other side of the Atlantic sought to discourage writers from pinning guilt on twins or doubles. But the ingenuity of crime novelists is such that they have been able either to abandon hoary old devices, or reinvent them pleasingly, while creating intricate and fascinating identity-based stories right up to this very day. Meanwhile talented practitioners have shown that tricky plot devices can be used as a springboard for subtle explorations of the ways in which character is bound up with notions of identity.

At a time when stories about cloning, identity theft and I.D. cards are seldom far from the headlines, the theme of 'crimes of identity' seemed a natural choice for this latest

ix

collection of stories to be published under the auspices of the Crime Writers Association. What I had not bargained for when I invited contributions from CWA members was the sheer volume of stories that came flooding through both post and cyberspace. In the ten years that have sped by since I took over editorship of the CWA's annual anthology, I cannot recall another theme that has been seized upon by so many established crime writers, from the UK and overseas. Quite an embarrassment of riches. My only regret is that constraints of space have meant that only a selection of the many excellent manuscripts that I received could be included here.

You will find in these pages stories, written specially for this volume, by those who have been awarded the CWA Diamond Dagger, as well as by an American Grand Master and last year's winner of the CWA Dagger for the best short story (Danuta Reah, who—fittingly in an identity-themed collection—features here as her *alter ego*, Carla Banks). The list of contributors includes such famous names as Peter Lovesey, Robert Barnard, Tonino Benacquista and Edward D. Hoch. But both the CWA and the publishers are keen to showcase the work of unfamiliar names and several authors represented here have not previously featured in CWA collections. A particular joy of editing the book has been to receive stories from writers—such as Yvonne

Eve Walus, Paul Freeman and Frank Tallis—whom I had not read previously, but whose work seems to me to have tremendous appeal. I do hope that readers coming to these or other authors for the first time will find their discoveries equally rewarding.

Over the years, CWA anthologies have appeared under the imprint of many of the most prominent publishers in the land: Hodder & Stoughton, Harper Collins, Victor Gollancz and Chatto & Windus to name a few. But this time we decided to link up with a relatively new yet exciting name in literary fiction, Manchester-based Comma Press. Comma is a not-for-profit publishing collective dedicated to promoting new fiction (and poetry) with particular emphasis on the short story. In a nutshell, Comma proclaims a commitment 'to a spirit of risk-taking and challenging publishing, free of the commercial pressures on mainstream houses.' There is surely a great attraction to many fiction lovers in the Comma credo:

'Something happens in good short stories which is unique to them as a form; the imaginary worlds they create are coloured slightly differently to those of the novel. Their protagonists are more independent and intriguing. The realities they depict more arbitrary, accidental and amoral. Comma believes British readers are missing out on something in their avoidance of the short story, and to make up for it we are currently the most prolific hardcopy publisher of short stories in the country.'

The prospect of linking up with a young and dynamic outfit with real zest and energy much appealed to the CWA committee. Several previous Comma publications have featured the work of CWA members and when Ra Page of Comma expressed enthusiasm for closer links, the opportunity was too good to miss. My thanks go to Ra and his team for their editorial input.

I would also like to express my appreciation of the support I have received from the CWA committee, chaired currently by Robert Richardson and previously by Danuta Reah. They work tirelessly to promote the genre and its exponents. I am especially grateful to all those who submitted stories, whether or not they eventually made the cut. Above all, I thank those who buy this book, for supporting a worthy and all too often neglected cause— the short crime story. It is a terrific form, full of potential. I hope readers agree with me that the contributors have exploited many of its possibilities to dazzling effect.

Martin Edwards
May 2006

Don't You Hate Having Two Heads?

Christine Poulson

He came to the Guggenheim Museum every time he visited Venice and it struck him as strange that he didn't remember seeing this sculpture before. It lay at his feet, more like a gigantic insect than the body of a woman. He was fascinated, yet he could scarcely bear to look. There was an arched backbone from which the ribs opened out like petals to the sun. Little breasts like grapes clustered above them. At one end of the spine, pipe-cleaner legs were splayed like those of a limbo-dancer. From the other end sprouted the neck, a long arc of vertebrae ending in a tiny head with a notch for a mouth. He looked at the title: *Woman with her Throat Cut* by Alberto Giacometti. He looked again at the sculpture. A little way down the neck was a second notch. This bloodless bronze was somehow more terrible than the goriest painting could have been.

It was as he turned away that he saw the girl for the second time.

He had first seen her going into the museum just ahead of him. He had admired the swing of her shoulder length hair as she leaned forward to buy her ticket. When she

1

straightened up, he realised that she was half a head taller than he was. He had always been attracted to tall women, particularly to those as elegant as this. She was wearing a fitted jacket in tan suede and high-waisted brown trousers that flattered a slender figure. And now there she was on the other side of the room gazing at a painting by Max Ernst.

He slipped off his wedding ring and pushed it deep into his trouser pocket. She was frowning a little, totally intent on the picture, and seemed not to notice as he drifted over in her direction. He glanced at the title: *The Robing of the Bride*. The painting was dominated by a monstrous figure with an owl's head. Its round eyes gazed out at the spectator with an expression at once enigmatic, melancholy, and predatory. Further down, the rich orange feathers fell into the folds of a floor-length cloak from which emerged the small breasts and the gently swelling stomach of a naked female body.

'Don't you hate having two heads?' the girl murmured.

Obviously she hadn't realised that he was standing behind her. He cleared his throat. The girl looked round. Her eyes widened. She was a brown-eyed blonde, an unusual combination. He felt a little thrill of excitement and apprehension.

'Has she got two heads?' he asked.

'Yes, look, right there. See that little face

2

peering out?' The girl had an American accent, light, attractive.

He moved forward so that he was standing next to her. He looked to where she was pointing. Just above the breasts, a tiny mask-like face was peering out through the feathers.

'So there is.'

' "Don't you hate having two heads?" is the title of another surrealist painting,' she said. 'It's by a British artist, Roland Penrose. It's kind of a joke.'

He smiled at her. 'I see that.'

She was older than he had thought. She must be about thirty, not really a girl at all. He was glad that she wasn't too young.

She pulled a notebook out of her bag. She gave him a brief smile and turned towards the seats in the centre of the gallery.

The encounter was over. At least for now.

He made his way through the central gallery past the Alexander Calder mobile, and pushed open the door that led down to the terrace overlooking the Grand Canal. The heat enveloped him. He hadn't expected the weather to be so good in late September. It was a real Indian summer.

He gave it ten minutes, then he headed back into the museum. She wasn't in the gallery where he had left her, nor in the garden. He felt a twinge of concern, but surely she couldn't have left yet. He strolled around, hoping at any moment to catch a glimpse of the bell of blonde hair, but he didn't come across her. After a while he gave up any pretence of examining the Picassos and the Jackson Pollocks and went through the rooms methodically, one by one. At last he had to admit defeat. She had gone and he had missed his chance. Stupid, stupid, stupid! Why hadn't he made a move earlier? It was a bloody nuisance just when he had psyched himself up to it. He had had so little practice, that was the trouble. He would have to mark this down to experience and start all over again.

First he would have a coffee. The museum cafe was crowded. Glancing round for a table, he saw at one end of the long narrow room a shallow flight of stairs and a sign to the Museum shop. He felt a flicker of hope. As he turned the corner into the shop, he saw her standing at the counter handing money to the sales assistant and receiving a small plastic bag, the kind that contains postcards. He breathed a sigh of relief. He moved deeper into the shop and paused by a rack of silk scarves. He looked back. She had moved away from the counter and was browsing among the books. He edged round to the racks of postcards and picked out several more or less at random. Now she was leaning over a cabinet of jewellery made from Murano glass. As he watched, she straightened up and walked towards the exit. He hastened to pay for the cards and followed her out.

At first he thought she was heading for the cafe, but she turned off into the ladies loo.

He hovered near the entrance to the shop and pretended to look at some books in a glass case. After a while she emerged and he hurried after her. He was just in time to see her sit down at a table. He looked around and felt like cheering. All the other tables were full. It couldn't have worked out better if he had planned it.

He walked over to her table.

'May I?' he said, gesturing towards the empty chair.

She nodded and smiled.

He ordered a cappuccino. When he caught her eye again, she stretched out a hand and said, 'Jessica David.'

There was a directness about her that threw him off balance: he almost gave his real name. Well, the Richard was real enough. But even as the word was on his lips he felt a moment of paralysing indecision. He hadn't prepared a false surname. And now she was looking into his eyes, waiting for him to go on.

'Richard Ford,' he said firmly, remembering a moment too late that this was the name of a well-known American writer. Still, it was a common enough name.

'Are you here on holiday?' he asked.

'No, I'm a student, a postgrad.'

Ten minutes later they were deep in conversation. She wasn't American at all, he

5

learned, but Canadian. She came from Quebec. He didn't have to feign interest. He had always wanted to go there.

They reached a natural pause in the conversation. The coffee had been drunk. For a moment neither of them spoke. She looked around. He knew she was preparing to leave.

'Is it too early for lunch?' he asked.

She hesitated and he thought he had lost her.

Then she said, 'Not at all too early. In fact I'm ravenous.'

They decided on ravioli stuffed with cheese and vegetables and an *insalata mista*. When Richard ordered a bottle of wine, Jessica did not demur.

As they drank the first glass, she told him about her research. She was looking at various surrealist artists from a feminist viewpoint.

'There were some women surrealists, weren't there?' Richard said, dredging his memory. 'Leonora Carrington, wasn't she one? And who did that cup and saucer lined with fur?'

'Meret Oppenheim. Oh sure, there are some marvellous women surrealists, but there's another side to it. I'm interested in the way women were silenced by surrealists.'

The waiter arrived with their food. Richard poured out another glass of wine for them both.

'What kind of thing have you got in mind?'

6

he said.

'There's a prime example here in this very museum.'

It was as if he could read her mind. He knew what was coming next.

'I'm thinking of that Giacometti sculpture,' she said. 'It's called Woman with her Throat Cut. There couldn't be a more effective way of silencing someone.'

As he cast around for something to say, his eye fell on the newspaper that Jessica had left on the empty chair between them. ASSASSINIO SUL CANAL GRANDE the headline read. Jessica followed his gaze.

'Have you heard about that?' she asked.

'I don't read Italian,' he said.

'It might not be in the English language papers yet. They only found the second body yesterday. Two in less than a week. The police think it's the work of the same person, so of course the press are making the most of it. There's a big spread about serial killers.'

'How does he?—I mean what happens—?'

'Cheese-cutter. They're garrotted with that thin strip of wire that you use to cut cheese.'

Richard felt queasy. His head was swimming. He poured himself a glass of mineral water. He told himself that he could walk away at any moment. He didn't actually have to do anything. This was just an experiment.

Jessica began to talk about the fellowship

she'd been awarded and the bad moment passed.

'So you've been here for a while?' he asked.

'Three months.'

'Where are you staying?'

'I've got a room in a flat. Not far away actually. And you?'

'A hotel in San Polo.' He didn't want to be more specific.

He looked down at the table and traced a pattern in a little puddle of spilled water.

'There's always plenty to do during the day, but it can be difficult in the evenings, can't it?' she said.

He looked up. She was smiling at him.

He said, 'I wonder . . . Maybe we could . . .'

'I'd like that.'

'This evening?'

'Why not?'

Now that this was settled, they began to talk of other things. Richard asked her if she'd like coffee. She said she would. He ordered it and then excused himself. In the gent's, he splashed cold water on his face and gazed at his reflection. He tried to see himself through Jessica's eyes. His hair and beard, both worn short, were greying and it suited him. Certainly he was more attractive now at forty than he had been at twenty. All the same he couldn't believe how easy it had been, almost too easy. He found himself feeling annoyed with her for being so ready to go off with a complete stranger. Didn't she realise how dangerous it was?

He went back into the cafe.

Jessica was gazing out into the garden with her back to him. As he approached their table, her head began to turn. And out of the blue it hit him: a wave of sheer panic. Because the head that swivelled towards him as if in slow motion wasn't the head of a woman. It was the owl-head of the bride in the Max Ernst picture. The feathery hair was made of real feathers, the brown eyes were round and unblinking, the little nose was a beak with a cruel curve at the tip. He closed his eyes. When he opened them, Jessica was herself again. She was looking at him with concern.

'What's the matter?' she asked.

He reached for a chair and lowered himself into it.

'Just suffering a bit from the heat.'

'Would you like a glass of water?'

He nodded and she poured one out for him.

'I need to go and freshen up myself,' she said.

As she walked away, it occurred to him that maybe it was the heat after all. That and the alcohol. The sky was completely overcast now and yet the heat was still building. He was sweating profusely. Or maybe these were the early symptoms of food poisoning. That cuttlefish he had eaten last night . . .

But whatever had caused that momentary

9

hallucination, he knew now that he couldn't go through with it.

The waiter appeared at his side and laid the bill on the table. He got to his feet, pulled out his wallet, and threw three twenty Euro notes on the table. He snatched up his packet of postcards, and ran out of the restaurant.

Ten minutes later he was on a vaporetto chugging up the Grand Canal towards the Rialto Bridge.

*   *   *

'Got your research done, darling?' Richard's wife asked.

She tossed her handbag and her newspaper onto the bed.

It was the following day and she had just arrived from Marco Polo airport. Richard had met her off the bus at the Piazza Romana and they had walked the short distance across a couple of canals to the hotel. On the way they had talked about the children, Marcus on holiday with friends for the first time and Emily at Pony Club camp. The success of Richard's last novel had made both the holiday and the Pony Club possible and had allowed Sarah to join him for a few days.

'Well, I did establish that it would be easy to pick someone up in the Guggenheim Museum.'

'I told you it would be. Art galleries and

10

museums are well-known intellectual pick-up places.'

Something in the silence that followed made her look round at him.

'You didn't actually pick someone up yourself?' She was laughing. 'You did, didn't you?'

'I did have lunch with someone,' he admitted.

'Attractive?'

'A lot of men would think so.'

'But you didn't?'

'She couldn't hold a candle to you.'

'Looks like I arrived just in time,' she said lightly. 'If you've done everything you need for the new book, maybe we can get down to some serious sight-seeing.'

He wasn't going to tell her that for a crazy half-hour he had contemplated taking it further. She might guess, but she wouldn't ask. She wasn't one of those tedious women who insist on having everything out in the open.

'I've found a very nice restaurant just off the Piazza San Margarita,' Richard said. 'I thought we'd go there for lunch.'

'I'll just do a bit of unpacking first and maybe have a shower.'

As she pottered around, he stretched out on the bed and glanced through the paper. He had more or less recovered from the day before. As he had alighted from the vaporetto, the heavens had opened. He had been soaked to the skin by the time he got to the hotel and to cap it all he was violently sick. He only just got back to his room in time.

He'd felt better by the evening and had slipped down to the hotel restaurant for a simple pasta. He had chosen a table at the rear of the restaurant. He couldn't rid himself of the fear that Jessica was cruising the hotels of San Polo looking for him. Thank goodness he had never before been seriously tempted to be unfaithful to Sarah. He didn't have the temperament for it. Better stick to fictional adventures and leave the real ones to bolder and more unscrupulous men.

Sarah had put her clothes away and had laid out her toiletries on top of the chest of drawers. Richard's belongings were lying scattered around and she began to tidy them up. Richard found this domestic activity comforting. He went on turning over the pages of *The Guardian* which had travelled with Sarah from East Midlands airport that morning.

His eye was caught by a headline. 'Death in Venice.' *Venetian police are denying that they have a serial killer on their hands*, he read, *even though the killer seems to have used the same modus operandi on both victims. Apparently they were garrotted with a length of cheese-wire. In both cases something was left by the body that leads the police to suspect that the killer is a visitor to Venice.*

'Really, Richard!' He looked up to see Sarah holding a plastic bag in one hand and a postcard in the other.

'Sorry—just let me—' His eyes went back to the newspaper.

Both men were around forty and of a similar physical type. Both were below average height. Both were married, but police do not discount a homosexual motive.

'My God! They weren't women, they were men!'

'Richard!'

And now he did focus on what Sarah had in her hand. It was a postcard of *Woman with her Throat Cut* by Alberto Giacometti.

'Why did you buy so many of the same thing?' she said with a moue of distaste. 'There must be a dozen of them. They're really gruesome.'

For a moment he was baffled. How had they got into his room? Then he understood. In his haste to leave the restaurant he had picked up the wrong plastic bag. Jessica had his Magritte and Alexander Calder postcards. He had . . . these.

'And that's not all. There's something else in here,' Sarah said.

She turned the bag upside down above the bed.

Richard knew what would be in there even before the gleaming, tightly-coiled length of cheese-wire landed on the counterpane.

13

The Document

Paul A Freeman

Marie-Anne and the children were out at
Grandma and Grandpa's. Good, thought the
Klansman—especially since the town historian
lay murdered in the hallway. All of which
proved how dangerous investigating someone
else's family history could be.

Sitting in his library, the Klansman stared at
the faded photograph the historian had
unearthed. What had the Klansman's great-
great-granddaddy been thinking of by jumping
the broom with a mulatto slave? The dead
historian had called the picture an important
historical document. The Klansman knew
other adjectives to describe it.

On inter-racial marriage, the Klan said,
'Once a drop of black paint gets into the white
paint tin, that paint will never again be white.'

Tears of shame welled in the Klansman's
eyes as he burned the photograph in an
ashtray. He could get rid of the picture and the
historian's body, but what to do about that
drop of black paint?

Les's Story

Stuart Pawson

Everybody calls me Les; always have done. Les Watson. I have a middle name but I hate it, never use it. It makes me mad the way parents give kids silly names, when they're too young to argue. Anyway, my mam says my middle name is Trouble. Then she always says: 'With a capital T.' That's why I'm here today, sitting in this room opposite a kid with a face like dogshit. He's wearing trainers from Matalan that most kids wouldn't be seen dead in. I'd rather go barefoot than wear them. Mine are Reeboks. His mam's with him, sitting there like it's her in bother, like it's her that's going to get all the grief.

156, The Headrow, second floor. That's where we're at, otherwise known as the Juvenile Court. My mam couldn't come because Tuesday is one of her days. She works part-time for a taxi company, sitting in the office taking phone calls, if you can call that work. It's cash-in-hand, she says, and jobs like that are hard to come by, so when they ask her to go in she can't say no.

I haven't got a dad. Well, I suppose I must have, somewhere, but I've only ever seen him once, years ago. This fellow called, one

15

Sunday, all nicey-nice with a bunch of flowers. They went down to the Lamb and Flag for a drink and came back late, when I was in bed. I could hear them giggling. Then it went quiet and then they had a row.

Except it was more like a fight than a row. They started smashing things and swearing. I thought he was going to kill her. I got up and put my clothes on, ready to jump out of the window if he came upstairs, after he'd killed mam, but I heard the door slam and mam called after him that he was some sort of a bastard and that was that.

She didn't get up until dinnertime next day, and she had a black eye and a fat lip. I asked her who the man was and she told me to mind my own business. I asked her again, a bit later, and she said: 'If you must know, that was your no-good father.' I'd only seen him when I opened the door. I'd have looked a bit harder at him if I'd known he was my dad. I hate being taken for granted like that. You'd have thought she'd have said come and meet your dad, or something.

It's all wood in here. Wood floor, wood walls, wood chairs, and it smells of polish. The chairs are all round the edge of the room and there's a little table in the middle of the floor with magazines on it and a few comics. There's just me and this other kid and his mam. My probation officer is supposed to be here but she's late. I nearly didn't come myself but I

16

missed last time and Gazz said that they put a warrant out for you if you miss twice and they can put you inside grisly Risley, wherever that is. Gazz is Gary Sutton. He used to be my best mate but he isn't now.

We were pals for ages. Sometimes, about once every term, I'd swear at the teacher and get suspended. Next day Gazz would do the same and we'd go roaming all over, sussing things out. I learned a lot from Gazz. Sometimes we didn't bother about being suspended and just bunked off. Kids do it all the time. If we were stopped by a cop or by security in the shopping centre we'd just say that it was a teacher-training day, or we were doing a project, and I'd smile at them. Everybody says I have a cheeky smile. They always believed us, never bothered checking.

We used to wander round the streets looking for things, mainly in the posh areas. You'd never believe how stupid some people are. They deserve to lose their stuff. We didn't start out thieving, when we were younger. In them days it was just a case of having some fun. We used to run over the flowerbeds in the park and pull up the trees they'd just planted. It sounds daft now, but we thought we were having a great time. Then we started nicking aerosols of paint from Wilkinson's and spraying our tags on the bus stop and the shelter in the station. Mine was a spider and Gazz called himself Big G, which was a laugh

17

because he's nearly as little as I am.

That was the first time I was caught. Somebody grassed on me and the community cop came round and found the aerosol of paint in the shed. It was called pyramid yellow, and was an exact match of the spider and bad word somebody had sprayed on the bookie's window. The cop said that the paint company had only made ten tins of pyramid yellow, and only one had come to Wilkinson's, so I had to admit it was me. That's what you call bad luck. I had to go to the nick and a cop in a white shirt told me that I'd better mend my ways or I'd be in big trouble. That's when I decided that making mischief was a mug's game. You got yourself into just as much trouble but didn't make anything out of it.

First thing we stole was a bike. This paper boy, a posh kid from the comprehensive, left it parked outside a house while he took the paper up the drive. We'd seen him do it loads of times. Gazz jumped on the saddle and I sat on the carrier, where his bag of papers was. We took it to the woods and rode round a bit on it, then hid it under some bushes. We threw all the papers in the ditch.

A week later we took it to Flash Harry's second hand shop and he gave us five pounds for it. I said it was mine but I had a stiff leg and couldn't ride it any more. I limped a bit as we went into the shop, but he always believes what you say. It was worth at least fifty, but he had a shop full of bikes and he said he couldn't get rid of them. Said it was the recession, whatever that is, and five was the best he could do.

In the summer we started knocking on doors. We'd follow an old person home from the post office, or sometimes we saw them out shopping, and if it was a hot day I'd ask them for a drink of water. Gazz would go round the back of the house and see if the door there was unlocked. It usually wasn't, but a window might be open, or the garden shed. We didn't have much luck with that, except for the time he managed to reach through a window and undo the latch. I spent ages drinking this cup of water an old man gave me, listening to him tell me about when he was at school and the teacher had a big stick that he belted you with if you got the answer wrong. I hate it how old people go on and on about how it was in the olden days. It makes me mad.

When I saw Gazz come down next door's path I said: 'Ta for the drink,' handed the cup back to him and walked off in the opposite direction. Gazz did well. He got a watch and seventy-three quid. There was a message in the watch that said the old man had worked at Kay's for fifty years. Blimey! Fifty years! Harry gave us a pound for it. Said it was no good with someone's name in it.

Then we started burgling. We'd look out for bottles of milk on steps, day after day. Houses with bushes in the garden were the best, where the neighbours couldn't see us. I'd knock at the door and ask if Jimmy was coming out to play if anybody answered, but nobody ever did because we were certain by then that it was empty. We'd either break a window at the back or I'd climb through one of those little ones if there was one open.

It was great when you were inside. Exciting, like nothing else. Some of the houses were really posh, with loads of good gear. Stuff I'd never seen before. We'd run through all the different rooms, pulling out drawers, rummaging through the clothes in the wardrobes. You should see some of the things they wore, like you see in magazines.

We couldn't carry the big stuff so we looked for money. That was the daft thing. They were rich people but they never had much money in the house. *Five pound millionaires*, Mam used to call them. So we took jewellery. There was always some of that, but it was never worth much. Harry said that rich people always had copies made and kept the real stuff in the bank. When we left a house we always put the plug in the upstairs sink and turned the taps on. Gazz said it would give the police something to think about, make it harder for them if the place was flooded. I didn't know what he meant but I'd have loved to see their faces when they came home.

Vicky Chadwick has just come in. She's my

20

probation officer.

'Hello Les,' she says, sitting down next to me. 'Sorry I'm late. I had to go to crown court with a PSR,' as if I knew what a frigging PSR was. 'How are you this morning?'

'OK.' She's wearing a coat and a big scarf that flaps about her shoulders, and she's puffing like she's been running.

'Good. So your mother couldn't make it then?'

'No, she had to go to work. She says there's six people wanting her job and if she misses she'll lose it.'

'I see. I've handed a report on your home circumstances to the clerk and explained things to the court. Now, Les, what you must do is look at the magistrate when he speaks to you and be polite. He's usually called Your Worship, but Sir will do. It is a man, this morning—Justice Montague. He's a stipendiary magistrate. That means he'll be sitting alone. I've asked for an extension to your probation, with the suggestion that we take steps to address your truantism and general behaviour. How does that sound to you?'

It sounds OK to me, except most of it goes over my head. *Home circumstances, sitting alone, address my truantism*, what does it all mean? She'd been talking to someone about me, as if I didn't exist. That makes me mad, that does, when they talk about you as if you

21

didn't exist. I don't care, as long as I don't get sent to grisly Risley. A tall woman comes in and speaks to the other kid's mam. They get up and follow her. Don't know what he did but I bet it was nothing much. He looked like a first offender, all scared. Mam says they'll be giving me an office down here if I come many more times.

It was the TV in the shopping centre that caught us. We'd nicked some T-shirts from Tog 24, good stuff, but the closed circuit TV recorded us shoving them under our coats. One of the security men recognised me and next time we went in they nabbed us. They took our fingerprints and Gazz's matched some they'd found on the taps in a house. Once they'd caught us Gazz said there was no point in denying it, so we confessed to eighteen similar offences. *Taken into consideration*, it's called, which means they don't really charge you with them.

I got probation and they gave Gazz community service, which was nearly as good as getting away with it. We kept on thieving. I would have stopped, but Gazz said that they wouldn't suspect us, now, as we had promised to go straight. I liked the sound of that, *going straight*. Made us sound like gangsters, which I suppose we were. We made a bit of money and he took it home for his dad to look after for us, until we were older and had proper jobs. We carried on just like before, except that now we wore gloves and sweat shirts with hoods.

I've done sex, just once. One night Gazz suggested that we go into Cut Price Booze, grab what we could and do a runner. We'd never done them before. We drank Special Brew now and again, but usually bought it. If you nick something like that you can't go back next day and nick some more, can you? It's a Paki shop, and Gazz always reckons that stealing from Pakis doesn't count. He says the police don't bother. So we looked round the shelves, minding our own business until the phone rang. Gazz nicked a bottle of whisky and I grabbed a bottle of wine and we ran for it. The Paki shouted after us but he didn't come running out.

It was Gazz's idea to go back to his house and have a party. I'd never been there. He said I could always stay the night, if I wanted. I thought about ringing mam but didn't bother. She didn't care what time I came home, and I'd stayed out all night before, in summer, sleeping in the woods.

Gazz's dad drank the whisky. I tried it but it was horrible. I didn't like the wine much, either, but they had some Special Brew in the fridge so I had that. We watched a video about two girls who go to London and meet this pop star, and laughed our heads off at all the rude bits.

I had four cans of lager. Every time I emptied one Gazza's dad got me another. 'Get it down you,' he kept saying. 'It'll do you good.' When the video ended I went upstairs to use the lavatory.

I'd just finished when I heard footsteps and the floorboards creaking outside the lav. I thought it was Gazz, but when I opened the door it was his dad. I smiled at him and stepped to one side, but he didn't go in. 'Here,' he said. 'Come in here, I want to show you something,' and he grabbed my arm and pushed me into the bedroom.

I didn't know what it was about at first, but he pushed me down on the bed and started undoing my jeans. I told him to stop but he didn't, and his breath stunk of whisky. He hurt me, really hurt me. When he'd finished he rolled off me and fell asleep, his arm across my back, pinning me down. I lay there, not daring to move until he started snoring. Snoring and stinking of whisky, that's how he was.

When I went downstairs Gazz was staring at the telly, his face turned away from me. He didn't look up and I didn't say anything, just went out and caught the last bus home. He did it deliberately, I'm sure of that. He took me home so his dad wouldn't do it to him.

Since then I've always gone about by myself. I never speak to Gazz, not even at school, which isn't difficult because he's never there. I stopped burgling and wandering about looking for places to do, but one day I thought of another scam, except this one was legal. More like a proper job than a scam.

I saw this old lady leaning on her gate, talking to a little black and white dog. The woman was really old and was getting her breath back before she walked down the garden path.

'Do you want me to take your dog for a walk, Missus,' I said, and gave her my smile. She told me that the dog was called Tigger and was getting a bit too much for her. I said: 'Don't worry about it, Missus. I'll take him for a walk.' So I did, and she gave me a fiver.

After that I went back every day; sometimes twice in the day, and she gave me a fiver every time. Until one day she only had a tenner, so I said it was OK, I'd take him for free next time, except when the next time came she gave me another tenner. These old people have more money than they know what to do with. I bought these trainers with the money, and some cargo pants. I told mam that I won them off a kid at school whose dad had bought them as a present when he came to visit but they didn't fit. She said: 'I'll believe you, millions wouldn't,' and that was that.

A few days later it all went wrong. I'd taken Tigger for a walk—down to the rec. where I sat on the swings for ten minutes while I had a fag and he had a run around—then took him back home again. The old woman came to the door when I knocked and looked surprised to see me. Usually she was waiting with my

25

money in her hand.

'Oh, it's you,' she said. 'I didn't realise Tigger was with you. I thought he was asleep in his basket.'

'That's all right, Missus,' I said. 'That'll be a tenner, please. Do you want me to take him tomorrow?'

She looked at me, all blank for a few seconds, then said: 'Oh, your money, of course,' and started humming and hawing and dithering about. 'I'll see what I can find,' she said, and went back inside, half closing the door.

I pushed it open and followed her. I thought she must have run out of cash, but she went into a drawer in this great big sideboard and pulled out a handbag. She didn't realise I was standing behind her. She fumbled with the fastening on the handbag and managed to open it and inside was the biggest roll of notes I've ever seen. There must have been hundreds of pounds.

I couldn't stop myself. I reached round her and grabbed the straps of the bag and pulled, but I wasn't quick enough and she clung on to it. I shouted at her to let go and called her an old cow, but she screamed back at me and we had a tug-of-war with the bag until Tigger joined in and started snapping and jumping up at me.

She shouldn't have screamed at me like that, and what with the dog jumping up and down and all the noise I really got my mad up. I swung her round, first one way and then the other, until the strap broke and she staggered backwards and fell over a chair. I went to pick up the bag but the dog snarled, showing these big yellow teeth, and bit me on the hand, so I turned and ran for it, slamming the door behind me so that it couldn't follow.

After that I didn't go out for a bit. I kept watching the news on telly and looking in the paper but there was nothing about an old lady being robbed. Mam asked me if I was poorly and I said I was, so she let me stay off school for a few days. Once I walked past the house but I didn't see anyone and I didn't go up the path. It was a shame, I thought, because it had been easy money.

I didn't see it in the paper but suddenly everybody was talking about it. An old lady had been found dead in her house but her dog was still alive, even though she'd been dead for about two weeks. I didn't even know if it was the same old lady, and anyway, she'd been alive when I left. She was really old, so she couldn't have had much longer to live.

Vicky Chadwick said: 'So how's school going, Les? Are you enjoying it?'

'No, it's boring,' I told her.

'What? All of it?'

'Yeah.'

'There must be something you like.'

'No, there isn't. Except school dinners

27

sometimes.'

'Have you made any new friends?'

'No.'

'Isn't there a teacher that you get on with?'

'No.'

Another kid came in with his mam and sat down where the other two had been. Vicky didn't say anything else after that. I wouldn't be here if it hadn't been for a kid at school. He was laughing at me because I had a Head bag, and according to him anything less than an Adidas is naff beyond belief. Head was not much better than Matalan. Then he said my mam ought to be able to afford one because she was on the game. I should have thumped him but he's bigger than me, so I went to the shopping centre, into JJB Sports, and decided that a Puma was what I needed. Except I'd never be able to nick one from there so I'd have to make some money and buy one.

The sun has come out and it's shining on me, making me blink. I didn't sleep much last night. Mam gave me a good telling off and told me to be polite and smile at the judge. Now I can hardly keep my eyes open. So I took a clock that's accurate for a million years from Debenhams, and an electronic chess game. Stuff that Flash Harry would give a good price for. 'Small but valuable, just like us,' as Gazz would say.

Except that they were waiting for me. As soon as I stepped outside the shop they

28

nabbed me, and here I am.

I don't want to go to grisly Risley. I don't want to go anywhere. I don't want to be sat here, opposite some other dumb kid, waiting to learn what's going to happen to me. Vicky Chadwick will say: 'Ah, well, Les, that's the best we could have expected,' and she'll go off to make a report in her nice warm office and then collect a bottle of wine on her way home and drink it with a posh dinner from Marks and Spencers. And I'll have to go home to mam and her boyfriends. She'll give me a fiver and tell me to stay out of trouble but not to hurry back and I'll go wander around town and have a hotdog from the stall outside the Las Vegas arcade.

I like watching the Simpsons on TV. They get into all sorts of bother but it's always all right because Homer gets them out of trouble. It's fiction, though, all pretend. I don't know anyone who has a dad like Homer. I wish I had.

I wish mam had come with me. I sniff and wriggle in my chair and Vicky puts her hand on my arm.

'Are you all right, Les?' she says, and I nod, staring down at the knees of my best jeans.

The tall woman has come back in. She's wearing a suit like someone in a TV ad for a posh car, but has clumpy shoes that don't go with it. She looks at the name on the paper she's carrying, then at the other kid and at me.

She decides it's me she wants and comes this way, smiling at Vicky and then at me, stooping so she doesn't have to say my name out loud.

'Lesley Jennifer Watson?' she asks,

God, I hate my middle name. 'Yeah, that's me,' I say. Here we go again.

The People in the Flat Across the Road

Natasha Cooper

It had been a ghastly day. I'd decided to work at home so I could finish the proposal for our biggest clients' new campaign. The copy was urgent, you see, because they'd pulled back the meeting by three days. My boss and I were due to make the presentation at ten next morning, and the designers were waiting in the office to pretty up my text and sort out all the PowerPoint stuff for us.

The trouble was I hadn't expected the interruptions: far more at home than in any office; and worse because of having no receptionists or secretaries to fend them off.

First it was the postman. Not my usual bloke but a temp, who couldn't tell the difference between 16 Holly Road, where I live, and 16 Oak Court, Holly Road, which is a flat just opposite. Even so, I shouldn't have shouted. It wasn't *his* fault he couldn't read much; or speak English either.

And he wasn't to know how many hours I've wasted over the past year redirecting all the mail I get that obviously isn't meant for me. Letters and packages with all sorts of names. I never pay much attention to the names once

31

I've seen they're not mine, so I couldn't tell you what they were now.

I opened one parcel by mistake, not having read the label before I ripped off the brown packing tape. Wondering why someone was sending me a whole bunch of phone adapters and wires and stuff, I turned the package over and saw it was meant for the flat. That was when I crossed the road and made my third attempt to introduce myself and sort it out. The funny thing was, you see, that in all the months I'd been dealing with their mail I'd never actually seen any of them. Once or twice there'd been a hand coming through the net curtains to open or shut a window, but that was all.

As usual, I got no answer, even though all the lights were on and there was a radio or TV blaring. I thought I heard their footsteps this time too, and voices, but I suppose it could have been my imagination.

Anyway, I was so cross they couldn't be bothered to do their neighbourly bit that I stopped bothering to take their mail across the road. I didn't even correct the wrongly addressed stuff (some of the senders missed out the Oak Court bit too; it wasn't only the postmen who got it wrong). Instead I'd scrawl 'Not Known Here', or 'no one of this name at this address' on the packages and envelopes, before stuffing them back into the post-box on my way to work. If the packages were too big, which happened occasionally, I'd stomp round to the Post Office on Saturday mornings and dump them at the end of the counter. It took much longer than carting them across the road and leaving them on the flat's doorstep, but it was way more satisfying.

Which maybe explains—though of course it doesn't excuse—the way I shouted at the poor stand-in postie this time round. He took three steps backwards and muttered some kind of apology, so of course I had to join in and explain I hadn't meant to yell.

Anyway, he was only the first. When it wasn't people collecting for charity—decent, kind, clean, well-spoken people, who didn't deserve to be glared at and sent away empty-handed—it was miserable, hopeless-looking young men trying to sell me ludicrously expensive low-grade dusters I didn't want. Or Jehovah's Witnesses. How was I supposed to flog my brain into producing light-hearted, witty, selling copy with all this going on? I was ripe for murder, I can tell you.

And then there was the small man in decorator's overalls, who had the cheek to ring my bell and tell me my neighbours had been complaining about my overhanging hedge. He offered to cut it back and take away the debris for some ludicrous sum. He got all the insults I'd been choking down all morning, and no apology, and I still think I was justified. Almost. At least I didn't lay a hand on him.

When I'd slammed the door in his face, I went back to my copy and re-read the pathetically little I'd managed to write. I had to delete the whole lot. You can imagine how I felt. I bolted some yoghurt for lunch and spilled most of it down my tee-shirt, so I had to change that and fling it in the washing machine, which wasted yet more time.

Then it was the end of the school day and there were shrieks from all the little darlings who'd been pent up in their classrooms for too long, and the exasperating heavy slap-slap of a football being kicked up and down the road. And chat from the little darlings' attending adults, who all seemed to want to stand right outside my front windows, either talking to each other or jabbering into their mobiles.

When they'd all gone and the street was blessedly quiet once more, the door bell went again. I shrieked out some filthy word or other (actually, I know quite well what it was, but I don't want to shock you) and ran to the door, wrenching it open and snarling, only to see my ten-year-old godson, looking absolutely terrified.

I apologised again, of course, and discovered he'd only come to return the tin in which I'd delivered his birthday cake. He's great and on normal days I enjoy his company. He has an interesting, off-beat take on the world, and his talk of school and sports and music often gives me ideas I can use for work when we're pushing children's products. So I had to ask him in and offer him some diet Coke, which was the only suitable thing I had in the house. Still looking scared, he shook his head and scuttled away like Hansel escaping from the wicked witch's gingerbread house.

I managed a quiet hour after that, and I had about twenty-five per cent of the copy written when the early evening crowd started, the meter readers, more charity-collectors, and then the party canvassers. Apparently we were going to have a by-election the next week. I eventually got down to real work at about eight, which was the time I'd have got back from the office on an ordinary day. I was spitting.

Still, I got the copy finished in the end—and it had just the right edgy-but-funny tone for the product. I was pretty sure the clients would like it. But when I saw it was half eleven, I knew the poor designers weren't going to be happy. I'd kept them hanging on for hours. I hoped they wouldn't be so angry they screwed up. We needed the presentation to *look* brilliant as well as sound it.

So I emailed my text to them with a genuine apology, and asked them to get it back to me by eight next morning with all the pix and whatever stylish tarting up they could manage. Then I copied everything to my boss, with an email to say I'd meet him at the clients' at nine forty-five. That would give me plenty of time to have the crucial six hours sleep and get my hair sorted and pick the best clothes to say it all: cool; money; efficiency; sexiness.

As you can imagine, I was pretty hyper by this time, so I took a couple of pills. Only over-the-counter herbal stuff. I think they're mainly lettuce, and the label on the packet always makes me laugh: 'Warning: May Cause Drowsiness'.

I was calming down a bit. I chased the pills with a glass of wine and a bit of bread and cream cheese with a smear of mango chutney, which reminds me of the sandwiches my mother used to make me when I was ill as a child.

So, fed, wined, and drugged to the eyeballs with lettuce, I took myself to bed. Just to be sure, I opened *The Unbearable Lightness of Being*, which hardly ever fails to send me to sleep. It did its stuff pretty soon, so I ripped off my specs and turned out the light, to find myself in that state where you fall hundreds of feet through the air, while still being plastered to the mattress. Heaven, really.

Through the lovely muzzy feeling, I thought I heard the phone ring once or twice. I ignored it and it stopped long before the answering machine could've cut in.

The next thing I knew I was floating on twinkling turquoise waves in warm sunlight with dolphins leaping in the distance and a raucous London voice yelling 'Go, Go, Go'. I'd barely got my eyes open when there was this almighty crash downstairs and thundering feet and cracking wood as my bedroom door burst open, spraying splinters and bits of the lock all over the place. I got chips of wood in my hair and all over my face.

I'd always been a coward. But I'd never been afraid before. Not like this.

I couldn't breathe. It was as if I'd been hit in the throat. My heart was banging like a pneumatic drill. And I thought I'd throw up any minute. Or pee in my bed.

The worst of it was I couldn't see anything much. There seemed to be dozens of sturdy thighs in jeans at eye level and stubby black things that looked like gun barrels.

It seemed mad. But it's what they looked like. All I could hear was panting: heavy, angry panting. Whatever they were going to do, I knew I had to be able to see, so I reached for the specs on my bedside table. A voice yelled at me to fucking stay where I was and not move. I couldn't. I mean, my arm was way too heavy. It crashed down on the table and knocked the specs to the floor with the lamp and my book. It also made them jam one of the black things nearer my face and yell at me to stay still.

It really was a gun.

Then a hand came nearer and grabbed the edge of the duvet. I hadn't got anything on under it, but that didn't strike me until they

37

ripped the duvet off me and let the cold air in. I twitched. I couldn't help it, in spite of the guns. But nothing happened. Except that one of them swore. I don't know what he thought he'd see under my duvet except me.

'*What*?' said one of the others. He moved his head a bit. At least, I think it was his head. All I could see was a kind of furry pink mass where his face must be. He raised his voice: 'What've *you* got?'

'Nothing,' called another man from further away. 'There's no one else. Only a kind of study, with a computer and filing cabinets and magazines and things.'

'Magazines? What magazines?'

'Women's stuff. *Cosmo*. *Vogue*. Things like that.'

He came closer and bent right down into my face. That's when I saw he had a dark-blue peaked cap with a chequered headband and POLICE in neat white letters.

I began to breathe again.

'God, you scared me,' I said and my voice was all high and quavery. I tried to toughen it. 'Can I have my glasses, please? And a dressing gown?'

'Don't move.' Three gun barrels came even closer to my face. And I heard the scrunch of glass. I don't suppose they did it deliberately, but one of them mashed my new Armani specs under his heavy great feet.

That was enough to make me more cross

38

than scared. Or maybe it was a reaction. Shock or something. Anyway, whatever it was, I forgot their guns and not having any clothes on and I just yelled at them, in a voice even my grandmother would have admired. And no one was grander than my grandmother.

'Stop being so damned silly. You've got the wrong sodding address, like the sodding post man. You want the people in the flat across the road. Now let me get up and get my dressing gown. And stop playing silly buggers with those *idiotic* guns.'

The nearest man took a step back and I knew I'd won. After a bit another of them handed me my dressing gown, smiling and nodding in a sloppy apologetic kind of way, like a bashful terrier. A minute ago he'd been holding a gun to my face; now he wanted to be friends? Mad.

Revisiting

Kate Ellis

Walter George examined his watch and saw that it was two o'clock. It was best, he thought, to arrive unannounced at the house of a stranger in daylight. In darkness people become suspicious, on their guard.

In the village he'd passed a pub called the Seven Stars—a small welcoming place with a climbing rose around the door: every serviceman's dream of Blighty. But Walter had resisted the temptation to stop there for a pint because he had no idea how the Bennetts would react to the smell of beer on his breath. The situation was delicate, and it was important to do the right thing; to create the right impression.

Walter straightened his tie. The ill fitting suit felt hot and uncomfortable after so many years in uniform. The men of Britain—those like him who'd survived the war—had all made their way home in new suits. Demobbed in pinstripes to face the anticlimax of victory. Perhaps when things improved, when he had money, he would buy himself something better.

He took the lane out of the village and a horse drawn hay cart passed him as he walked.

The young woman at the reins smiled, wishing him good afternoon, and Walter returned her greeting. She was pretty, perhaps a land girl who had stayed in her post after hostilities had ended, or maybe a farmer's daughter. For a few seconds Walter wondered whether to ask her if she knew Gappling House. But he decided to err on the side of caution: there was always a chance that such an enquiry might spark off gossip in the neighbourhood. He knew only too well how inquisitive small communities could be and the last thing he wanted to do was draw attention to himself.

After walking some distance in the warm, late August sun, he reached a gate and pulled a crumpled piece of paper from his pocket. It looked as if he'd found the place at last. And it was isolated. Isolation suited his purposes well.

Gappling House was situated well away from the village, down a long drive and half concealed by trees. A private place. The oak sign bearing the name of the house in bold letters looked freshly painted. People like the Bennetts maintained standards . . . even in wartime. Charles Bennett had never spoken much of his family's wealth. But then the truly affluent have no need to boast.

Walter rehearsed what he would say. He knew he had to make a good impression so that his account of his close friendship with Charles on the base wouldn't be doubted. But the more he rehearsed his story, the more unconvincing it sounded. Walter stood there by the tall stone gatepost, momentarily distracted by the noise of quarrelling crows in a nearby tree, and pulled his wallet from his inside pocket. He took out Charles's photograph and the sight of the open, handsome face brought memories flooding back.

Charles Bennett had been six feet tall, fair haired and good looking with the kind of nonchalant charm that resulted from a public school education. Walter had envied the young pilot these gifts endowed by nature and birth. But all the privilege in the world couldn't keep death at bay.

His lines rehearsed, Walter took a deep breath and began to walk up the drive. His new shoes were starting to pinch but he strode forward. Appearing confident was half the battle and he told himself over and over again that the story he was about to tell Charles's bereaved parents was the truth and nothing but the truth. If his resolve wavered they would realise he was lying. And that was a risk he couldn't take.

Half way down the drive he stopped to look at the house. It was the sort of house built for Victorian vicars or prosperous farmers—large but not over-grand—but to Walter, who had been born in a terraced street in lower middle class suburbia, it seemed as grand as a stately home. Charles's world had been so different from his own.

As he approached the front door, he wondered whether Charles's family would have servants. But he had heard that the war had put a stop to that sort of thing. Menservants had signed up for the forces and the women had gone into munitions factories or the land army. The old certainties, the old hierarchies were fading fast and the thought gave Walter some satisfaction.

He gave the iron bell pull next to the studded oak door a strong tug and waited, his heart beating rapidly. When there was no answer he tried again. But the jangling inside the house was followed by silence. Perhaps they were out, he thought. Or away somewhere. If that was the case, he'd have to rethink his plans.

He was about to retrace his steps down the drive when he heard a bolt being drawn back, the noise sharp as a gunshot against the soft sounds of the countryside. He swung round, straightened his back and cleared his throat. The show was about to begin.

The door was opened by a tall man in his sixties with a tanned complexion and abundant grey hair. He wore a shirt and tie and his hands were busily buttoning up his waistcoat, as though the arrival of a visitor had caught him off his guard.

'Mr Bennett?' Walter asked, inclining his head politely.

'Yes.' The man sounded a little wary.

'We've never met but I was a friend of Charles. I've come to tell you how sorry I am about . . .'

Walter detected a split second of doubt in the man's eyes. Then he held out his hand to Walter. 'Of course. Thank you so much for coming. Have you travelled far?'

This was the question Walter had been hoping for. 'Yes, I have as a matter of fact. When we were demobbed I travelled from the base in Lincolnshire home to Liverpool. But I found my house had been bombed and . . .' He paused here, took a clean linen handkerchief from his pocket and dabbed his eyes. 'My mother and my sister . . . Doodlebug landed on the shelter.' He patted his eyes again to make his point.

The man's wariness seemed to disappear. 'My dear chap, come in. Please. I'll ask my wife to make some tea.' His voice was posh like a radio announcer's . . . like Charles's. He stood aside and Walter stepped into the hallway, taking in his surroundings. The walls were hung with paintings, mostly watercolours of rural scenes, and there was a thick Persian carpet on the polished parquet floor. Mr Bennett led the way to the drawing room and invited Walter to sit on a worn chintz sofa before excusing himself.

As soon as he was alone Walter seized the chance to explore the room. A mirror hung

44

over a grand fireplace decorated with blue and white delft tiles. There were more paintings on the wall here—oils in heavy gilt frames—but there were no portraits and no family photographs, not even on the grand piano that stood near the window. Walter walked over to the piano and examined the sheet music propped up on the open lid. He smiled when he saw it was an American popular song. 'The Boogie Woogie Bugle Boy from Company B'. Somehow he hadn't thought of Charles's parents as the popular song sort. But sometimes people can surprise you.

There was money here, he could tell. And as Charles had been an only child, there would be nobody, as far as he knew, to ask any questions. On the journey down to Devon, Walter had examined his conscience briefly before concluding that in desperate times different rules apply.

His thoughts were interrupted by the return of Mr Bennett. Behind him, twisting a lace handkerchief in her thin fingers, was a tall woman with sharp features. Walter remembered his manners and stood up in the presence of a lady. She looked uneasy, he noticed, but this was hardly surprising: she had lost her only son in the war and grief can manifest itself in many forms. Charles Bennett had died a hero's death in a dog fight over the English Channel—one of the RAF's finest. But noble circumstances don't make death any

45

easier. Death is death, whatever its guise.

'My dear, this is Walter George. He served with Charles. You were a pilot, Mr George?'

Walter felt his cheeks burning. 'Ground crew,' he replied. At least this wasn't a lie. 'But I knew Charles well. I do apologise for turning up unannounced but Charles did say that I should visit you and . . . '

'Of course, my dear chap. We're delighted to see you. Any friend of Charles and all that . . . ' Mr Bennett chuckled awkwardly as his wife flopped down. She looked shocked. Walter assumed that his arrival had reminded her once more of her loss. He glanced at her and felt a sudden pang of guilt.

'Charles was a wonderful man,' Walter said with all the sincerity he could muster. 'And so brave. Quite fearless. He spoke of you a lot.'

The Bennetts exchanged glances. 'Really?' Mr Bennett said casually.

'Yes,' Walter replied with a confidence he didn't feel. He had never actually heard Charles mention his parents. All he knew about them came from Bill Stebs who had gathered Charles's personal effects on his death to give to the C.O. who would return them to his next of kin. Stebs hadn't been able to resist reading his letters—he'd been a nosey bastard, a real old woman and a terrible gossip. Walter had asked to see the letters and, for the price of a few cigarettes, Stebs had agreed. Walter had fixed their contents in his

46

mind . . . every word. And when desperate times came he'd hardened himself to use the memories, those precious memories, to his own advantage.

He sipped his tea, making polite conversation and, as the time passed, he was invited to join the Bennetts for dinner. Then, when he made no move to leave, politeness obliged them to invite him to stay the night.

Which was exactly what Walter George had intended.

*   *   *

It was all going to plan. Walter sensed from the Bennetts' stiff manner that they would rather be left alone but he did his best to ingratiate himself by treating them with scrupulous politeness and charm. He was sure that if he persisted, he'd soon have his feet well and truly under the table, as his mother used to say. And besides, he felt close to Charles here.

He had visited Charles's room where he'd sat on the bed, staring at the model aeroplanes that hung from the ceiling—a terrible foretaste, Walter thought, of the manner of his death. It was a boy's room rather than a man's. But then Charles had been twenty-one when he died . . . hardly a man at all.

The evening of stilted conversation and awkward glances passed slowly and the next morning Walter started to feel a little

47

uncomfortable about the burden he was placing on the thin, monosyllabic Mrs Bennett. He had seen no servants and he realised that his presence was probably causing a lot of domestic inconvenience. So at eleven o'clock he excused himself, saying he'd find something to eat in the village. Mrs Bennett concealed her relief well but Walter knew he had to avoid abusing her hospitality. The Bennetts had to want him there. They had to accept the man they thought of as their son's friend . . . not resent his presence.

The village lay a mile away along narrow country roads. It was a fine day and Walter set out, enjoying the music of the skylarks in the fields that lined his route. The landlady of the Seven Stars was happy to make him a ham sandwich and he sat down by the unlit fire, near to an elderly man who looked at him expectantly.

'Now then, my lover,' the man said, smacking his lips.

Walter looked at him startled, unused to the Devon greeting. Then he gathered his thoughts and wished him good day, concluding that it would do no harm to invite the old boy to join him in a drink, an invitation that was accepted eagerly.

'Not seen you round these parts before,' the man began, looking Walter up and down.

'I'm staying with Mr and Mrs Bennett at Gappling House.'

The man took a long drink from his tankard and put it down. 'I hear they keep 'emselves to 'emselves these days. Ever since their lad died.'

'I was a friend of their son's.'

The man's expression gave nothing away.

'Like I said, they keep 'emselves to 'emselves. Don't come in the village no more.'

'I suppose they find it hard . . . facing people after losing . . . '

The man nodded and no more was said on the subject.

After one drink, a sandwich and some less than sparkling conversation about the weather, Walter excused himself and left the pub, stepping out into the sunlit village street. The village, as far as he could see, possessed few attractions for a young man with time on his hands and yet he felt reluctant to return to Gappling House. Apart from the pub, there was only one other place that might be of interest to an outsider and that was the little medieval church. So, for want of anything more entertaining on offer, Walter wandered through the lych gate and made his way up the tomb-lined path.

He opened the great oak door and, as he stepped inside, his eyes adjusted to the gloom and he realised he wasn't alone. A young woman wearing a cotton frock and a pink silk headscarf was kneeling in one of the front pews, deep in prayer. When she heard his footsteps she looked up nervously and, after a few moments, she stood up and wished him good afternoon.

Walter saw that she was beautiful with raven hair and blue eyes. And he was sure he'd seen her before somewhere but he couldn't think where. He gave her a shy smile which she returned. 'I'm sorry to disturb you,' he said. 'I'm visiting some people nearby and I thought I'd take a look around.'

'So we're both strangers,' she said, blushing. 'I hoped you'd be a local. I'm looking for a place called Gappling House.'

Walter stared at her, stunned, as though she'd hit him. He had to think quickly. 'Er . . . you're looking for Mr and Mrs Bennett?'

'Yes. I've met them before. I was a friend of . . . of their son.'

This was getting worse. 'Charles? I knew him too. I served on the base with him.' It was too late to go back now so he knew he had to make it sound convincing. 'I was down this way and I thought I'd call in to give them my condolences . . . pay my respects.'

The young woman smiled. 'That's very thoughtful. I'm sure they'll appreciate it. It's so hard when people ignore you because they don't know what to say, isn't it? When my husband died . . . ' She stopped in mid sentence, as though she feared she'd said too much.

'I'm sorry.' Walter said automatically. 'I thought you said you were a . . . a friend of

Charles?' He had to find out where this woman fitted in. Her arrival was something he hadn't bargained for. And it had come as a shock.

'It's a long story,' she said with a sad smile.

Walter assumed a sympathetic expression. 'I'm a good listener. And sometimes it's easier to confide in a stranger; someone who won't judge. You have my solemn word that whatever you tell me will go no further. And who knows, we may never meet again.'

The young woman slumped down in the pew and Walter sat beside her, his head inclined slightly, like a priest ready to hear her confession.

'I suppose it'll do no harm to tell you. The truth will be out soon anyway. I'm on my way to tell Charles's parents.'

'You know the Bennetts well?'

'I wouldn't say I know them. Charles met them in Lincoln once when he had a few days' leave: I happened to be in town and when I bumped into them he introduced me and we made polite small talk for a few minutes.' She twisted her handkerchief in her fingers. 'I honestly don't know how they'll take it.'

'Why don't you tell me the whole story and I'll give you my opinion.' Walter smiled, his most charming smile.

She took a deep breath and held out her hand. 'I'm Sally Fenner, by the way.' Once the formalities were out of the way, she began to

51

recount her tale in a hurried whisper. 'My husband was posted abroad so I went home to help my father run the pub near the base. The Blacksmith's Arms. You must know it. All the pilots went there—that's how I met Charles. He was a real charmer.'

'You're right there,' Walter said with feeling, realising why her face seemed familiar. He must have seen her behind the bar when he had followed Charles in there that one time; the time he remembered so well.

She studied Walter's face. 'I don't recall seeing you at the Blacksmith's.'

'That's probably because I was ground crew. We tended to drink elsewhere. The Oak Tree usually,' Walter replied smoothly, careful to be vague.

Sally nodded. 'Anyway, to cut a long story short, me and Charles . . . '

'I see. Well, he was a charmer like you said.'

She blushed and pushed back an imaginary strand of hair. 'That's not all. I have a son, Derek. He's a year old now.'

'Really?' Walter wondered what was coming and he was suddenly afraid.

'My husband's only just been confirmed dead so I couldn't come here before. I had to keep up the pretence. But I want Charles's family to know the truth about me and Charles. I've come to tell Charles's parents that they have a grandchild.'

Walter opened his mouth but no sound came

out.

Sally looked anxiously into his eyes. 'You're shocked?'

Walter shrugged. 'There was a war on. Who am I to judge?'

She gave him a shy smile.

Walter said nothing for a few moments, unsure how to play this new development. 'Do you think you're doing the right thing, telling the Bennetts?'

She stood up. 'Charles was their only son. I think they should be told, don't you? I might as well get it over with. Will you walk with me?'

Walter shook his head. 'It's probably best if you go alone. And besides, I've got things to do.'

It wasn't until the next morning that Sally Fenner's body was found a mile from the village, floating in the River Tavy.

*   *   *

There was no identification on the body and nobody in the village knew who she was. A mystery woman. Walter visited the Seven Stars shortly after the body was found and discovered from his new found drinking companion that the police had no clue to her identity. They were looking for her handbag: her ID card and ration book had to be somewhere. Walter knew it would be the talk

53

of the village for a while. Until the gossips found a fresh topic to rake over.

Sally Fenner's death had made things considerably easier for him. He asked the Bennetts whether they'd seen the dead woman, careful not to mention her connection with Charles, but they said they knew nothing. She had never arrived at Gappling House.

When Walter had been with the Bennetts for a couple of days he sensed that his welcome was wearing thin and he reckoned it was time to move on to the next stage of his plan. A little light blackmail would surely produce the desired result.

As always he was careful to maintain the charm. Even when he hinted that Charles had a dark secret that only he knew—and claimed that he was desperate to secure some capital to start up his own business—he said it with a winsome smile. But the Bennetts didn't seem to catch on and Walter concluded that, so far, he'd been too subtle.

He lay back enjoying the Indian summer, sipping Mrs Bennett's home made lemonade and thinking of Charles Bennett. He'd been arrogant and beautiful and Walter had admired him from afar—looked but never touched. How easy it would be to ascribe his own secret to Charles. Now that Sally Fenner was dead, who was to contradict Walter when he told the Bennetts that their son preferred the company of men to women? They would surely pay—and pay well—to ensure that such a slur on Charles's memory was never repeated. It would be such a shame if Charles's secret came out and besmirched his perfect memory, wouldn't it? A scandal would be so distressing. People don't like their heroes to have feet of clay.

They could hardly prove that it had been Walter who had desired Charles, not the other way around—secretly of course as that sort of thing was never mentioned in the manly world of the base. Charles, the god-like hero, had hardly noticed the humble aircraftsman's existence, but that wouldn't be Walter's version of events. Getting money from the Bennetts would be his revenge. The revenge for being treated as a nobody by the man he most desired.

That afternoon the Bennetts took the car out to visit the shops in Tavistock and Walter, alone in the house at last, took immediate advantage of their absence. As soon as the car disappeared from sight down the drive, he began to explore the corners of the house he hadn't yet seen. He sat for a while in Charles's room, daydreaming about the man he had longed to call his friend, if not his lover, before taking a perfunctory look around the other bedrooms and climbing up to the attic where he found a pile of framed photographs of Charles and other people; a middle aged couple, an uncle and aunt perhaps. There were no photographs of the Bennetts: but then some people dislike having their picture taken.

Walter found the house a little disappointing. He discovered a large sum of money and a cheque book in Mr Bennett's study but he didn't touch them because he knew their absence would be noticed and the last thing he wanted to do was arouse suspicion at this stage. It seemed that the Bennetts had no secrets—at least none that were of any use to him—so he would have to use his insinuations about Charles to achieve the desired result. A fat payment to keep quiet. It was so fortunate that Sally Fenner was dead: she might have ruined everything with her talk of a grandchild.

Walter made his way downstairs and wandered into the kitchen garden where fruit and vegetables grew in lush abundance. Mr Bennett certainly had green fingers, he thought as he made for the large wooden garage that stood near by. As he entered he saw a row of petrol cans lined up against the far wall. Someone had been buying from the black market. Perhaps the Bennetts weren't so upright and respectable after all.

He put his hand to his nose. There was an unpleasant smell in the garage; rotting vegetation perhaps; certainly not petrol. Then the sight of an Alvis parked at the far end of the garage drove everything else from his mind. Walter walked over to the car and began to stroke the dusty metal in admiration. It was a beauty, he thought, wondering whether it had belonged to Charles. The door was unlocked so he climbed into the driver's seat, placing his hands gently on the steering wheel like one caressing a lover.

He leaned over and opened the glove compartment, wondering what secrets it held, and a small handbag tumbled out onto the passenger seat. Walter's heart began to race. He had seen the bag before. He grabbed it and opened it, letting out an involuntary gasp when he saw the name on the ration book inside.

After a few stunned seconds he climbed out of the car and closed the door gently, wondering how long he had before the Bennetts returned. His imagination began to supply the story. Sally Fenner had arrived at Gappling House and had told her story to Charles's parents. Then something had happened—an accident perhaps—and they had put her body in the river. Or perhaps Mr Bennett had lost control when he learned of the disgrace his son had brought to the family name. Or perhaps she had sat in Charles's car one last time, leaving her bag there, before committing suicide in the river when his family had rejected her and her child. There were so many possibilities. But, whatever the truth was, the Bennetts would be only too happy to buy his silence.

Carrying Sally's bag, he crept out of the

garage. He would tell the Bennetts in the nicest possible way to pay up or he'd go to the police. This was his golden opportunity to milk them dry.

He walked towards the big double doors, smiling to himself. Then something caught his eye. Let into the floor where the Bennetts' car had stood was a wooden trapdoor; an inspection pit. And something was peeping out of the edge . . . a tattered fragment of pink cloth. Curious, Walter walked over and raised the trap door.

He was quite unprepared for the stench of rotting flesh and the sight of two half decayed corpses, a man and a woman, lying at the bottom of the pit.

He dropped Sally's bag, stumbled from the building and vomited into a flowerbed. Then, hardly aware of what he was doing, he ran into the house and telephoned the police, careful not to give his name, before dashing upstairs to fetch his things. There was no way he was staying in that house. Not now.

But when he reached the front door he realised it was too late. The Bennetts' car was drawing to a graceful halt in front of the garage and he had left the inspection pit open, its grisly contents on view. Walter could talk his way out of most things but there was no way charm would get him out of this one.

There was nothing else for it. He'd have to face his enemy, something he'd never had the chance to do when the war was on.

Bennett was approaching, a false smile fixed on his face. His wife stalked behind, her thin lips pressed together, her hard eyes narrowed to slits.

Walter saw the man was holding a gun. And it was pointed straight at his heart. 'Who are they?' he asked, his voice shaking. He knew he had to keep them talking.

'Violet and Cuthbert Bennett,' the man answered, the gun still aimed at Walter's chest. The announcer's accent was gone now, replaced with a rough London twang.

'So I take it you're not Charles's parents? And, er . . . if that's the case, do you mind telling me who you are?' He spoke calmly, playing for time.

The man gave a bitter smile. 'If you must know, I was the gardener and my good lady wife here was the housekeeper. We answered an advert when their old servants signed up. They should have been more careful but they were desperate. Helpless they were without someone to fetch and carry for 'em.' He grinned. 'We reckoned we'd like a slice of the high life so when they lost their son and it came out that they had no other relatives we thought, why not?'

'You shot them?'

'It was quick. Didn't know what had hit 'em. You were going to be next if you didn't move on sharpish. The last thing we wanted was a bloody lodger.'

The gun clicked and Walter searched frantically for the next question, the one that would delay this killer until the police arrived. But then they would probably only send the village bobby on a bike. He was staring down the barrel of a gun, staring at death as he had never stared at in all the years of the war. And he was afraid.

'What about Sally Fenner? I take it you killed her too.'

'She'd met the bloody Bennetts, hadn't she? Guessed something was up as soon as she clapped eyes on us. I knocked her out with my pistol then dumped her in the river. I wanted it to look like the silly cow had killed herself.'

Walter took a step backwards, racking his brains for the next question. But his mind was blank.

The woman spoke. 'Just kill him, John. Get on with it.'

'I've called the police,' said Walter in desperation.

As the couple looked at each other, Walter seized his chance. He rushed at the man, knocking the revolver from his hand, just as the black police car appeared around the corner.

*   *   *

The arrest had been made. It was over.

The couple—real names John and Freda Martin—had made an abortive attempt to escape by running off through the garden. But they'd soon been apprehended and in the end they had yielded to the inevitable, going with the police quietly, knowing they would face the noose.

'We'll need a statement from you, sir,' a constable said to Walter.

He noted that he had been addressed respectfully: but then why shouldn't he be? As far as the police knew, Walter was merely an old friend of the Bennetts' late son come to pay his respects . . . almost a victim himself. He gave his statement and realised that, apart from his account of his relationship with Charles Bennett, he hadn't really had to lie.

The police were busy in the garage when Walter excused himself and returned to the house, saying he wanted to fetch his things and book into an inn for the night. He asked if it was alright to take his car out of the garage: he realised the building was a crime scene but he really did need the car. The policeman in charge said he didn't see why not.

As soon as Walter was alone in the house he began his search and found Charles's ration book and ID papers, kept in a bureau by his parents who probably hadn't been able to bring themselves to throw away this fragile link with their dead son. Putting them in his top pocket, Walter ran upstairs to get his things, but not before taking the money and cheque book he'd discovered in the study: C Bennett—probably Charles's father, Cuthbert. Perfect.

As he drove away in the Alvis that he had convinced the young policeman standing guard was his, he began to make his plans. C Bennett. The name would look good above a shop. A car showroom maybe.

By nightfall he had reached Bristol and the following day he was in Yorkshire. Walter George was gone forever.

The Rock

Edward D Hoch

Linda O'Toole had been in Gibraltar only a few hours when a rumpled little man stopped her in the lobby of the Rock Hotel and asked, 'Pardon me, but are you Laura Nostrum?'

'That's right,' she agreed. 'Can I help you?'

'I'm Liam Fitzhugh with the London *Daily Mail*. Do you have any comment on the Internet news story stating that you're an undercover agent for the Central Intelligence Agency?'

Linda gave him her brightest smile. 'I can't imagine what you're talking about. I'm here representing Osage Investment Corporation at the Casino Conference.'

'Then you deny any involvement with the CIA?'

'I certainly do. If you'll excuse me now, I have a meeting to attend.' When he showed no interest in stepping aside she walked around him and out of the hotel.

*   *   *

Gibraltar, a slender peninsula extending south from Spain and separated from it by a kilometer-wide neutral zone, might have

63

seemed an odd venue for the first worldwide casino conference, but among the attending nations it seemed both centrally located and relatively independent of foreign influence. True, Gibraltar was an overseas territory of the United Kingdom, but 'overseas' was the operative word. Its reputation as an international conference center was well earned. This was not the same as having such a conference in London or Las Vegas or Monaco, where the influence of local casinos could well control the agenda. Gibraltar had only two land-based casinos, both quite a bit smaller than the average American ones, and both located on Europa Road. One was in the Rock Hotel where Linda was staying, a long white multi-storey building that blended well with its surrounding gardens.

At the nearby theatre where the meeting was taking place she stopped at the registration desk and identified herself as Laura Nostrum. The ID badge was waiting for her. She pinned it on her jacket and started into the auditorium, then changed her mind and headed for the ladies' room instead. Inside one of the stalls she took out her cell phone and punched in a familiar number in a Paris suburb. When the connection was made she didn't speak but merely punched in another series of numbers. She received an answering beep, closed her cell phone and left the room.

Back at the theatre the first man she met

was a bearded Frenchman named Pierre Zele. He carried an ivory-knobbed cane, leaned down for a better look at her ID badge and introduced himself. 'I am here on behalf of the casino at Monte Carlo,' he told her, 'and I am president of our association this year. I trust this little conference I helped organize can accomplish something, Miss Nostrum.'

'Please call me Laura. I represent Osage Investments.'

'They are one of your Native American tribes. No?'

'Well, there is an Osage tribe, but we have no connection with them. We have a proposal to make regarding the investment of casino profits. I'll be addressing your conference tomorrow morning.'

Pierre Zele eyed her with new interest, studying her ID badge as if to memorize the name. She wondered if he had seen the Internet report the Daily Mail reporter had mentioned. 'I will be listening with interest,' he promised, and turned away.

The afternoon sessions were under way when she entered the theatre, but progressing slowly as remarks were translated into English and French. After some thirty minutes she exited, along with a slender young man whose nametag read Michael Patrick, Ireland.

'Gets a bit boring, doesn't it, sitting through those translations?' he observed as they reached the outer lobby. 'They should use

65

simultaneous translators like the UN.'

'That would be more expensive,' she told him, glancing again at his nametag. 'You're Irish.'

'Guilty. Since we both ducked out of there together, could I buy you a drink at the hotel bar?'

'Sure, why not?'

They walked around the corner and up the hill to the Rock Hotel. Though the main casino didn't open until nine in the evening, the slot machines were in operation from noon on. Their familiar clanging could be heard even in the hotel's cocktail lounge. 'Is this your first trip to Gibraltar?' he asked after they'd ordered whiskey and water.

'It is! I'm anxious to see the apes.'

Michael Patrick smiled at her. 'They're actually tail-less monkeys known as Barbary Macaques. British sailors brought the first ones here after the Royal Navy captured the stronghold in 1704. There are more than 160 now, each one named at birth, but they almost died out during World War II and Churchill famously took steps to insure their survival. Tradition has it that when the apes were gone the British would be gone too.'

'You know a great deal,' she said, sipping her whiskey. 'Apes or monkeys, I'd like to see them.'

'That's easily arranged. They're in two areas. The best for viewing is the Apes' Den at

66

Queen's Gate, right up the hill behind this hotel. And surely you'll want to view the Rock itself from the observation deck. We can reach it by cable car. I'd be pleased to give you a tour tomorrow.'

She shook her head. 'I have to read a paper at the morning session.'

'Perhaps later, then.'

'I thought casinos were still illegal in Ireland. What brings you here?'

'Commercial casinos are illegal, but there are a number of private members' clubs throughout the country. We have seven in Dublin alone. I manage one of the smaller ones.' He passed her his card, with a lucky clover embossed in green. 'If you're ever up that way, come see our place. I'll get you members' privileges.'

'Thank you, kind sir,' she said, tucking the card away in her purse. Glancing toward the bar, she spotted the British journalist, Liam Fitzhugh, eyeing her. Time to move on, she decided. 'And thanks for the drink. I have to go now.'

Later that evening, after the full casino was in operation, she wandered in and spent some time at the roulette wheel. It was American style roulette, with both the zero and double zero. She noticed the Frenchman, Zele, avoiding the table.

'Are you enjoying yourself, mademoiselle?' a handsome foreign gentleman asked after she'd won on three spins in a row.

'I am indeed, but I'm no mademoiselle. I'm an American.'

'Ah, yes!' He glanced at her ID badge which she'd neglected to remove. 'Laura Nostrum. I am Bert Stein.'

'German?'

He smiled. 'Born there, but I've lived in Spain for thirty years.'

'Are you attending the casino conference?'

'Yes,' he replied, remembering to take the ID badge from his pocket. 'It is a good excuse to visit the Rock, which should belong to Spain.'

'You want Gibraltar back?'

'Most certainly,' he said with conviction. 'It is the most famous rock in the world, even more famous than Ayers Rock in Australia. There have been referendums from time to time, but always the people vote to remain a British dependency.'

She placed a few chips on the red and lost. 'I guess my luck just changed. I'd better quit while I'm ahead.'

'If you'd like a tour of the Rock—'

'Thanks. I've already had an offer.'

*　　　*　　　*

In the morning the theatre was filled as the casino session got under way in earnest. Pierre Zele said a few words by way of introduction, and then it was Linda's turn. She came directly to the point. 'I'm here on behalf of Osage Investments, a small international company with big plans. It seemed fitting that this first casino conference be held here in Gibraltar, where we can actually look across from the rock to the poorest continent, just thirteen kilometers away. Africa needs our help. It needs our money. There can be no better use for the billions of dollars and pounds and euros that would otherwise be reinvested in newer and larger casinos.'

She went on from there, making a passionate case, but already she was aware of some eyes glazing over, some hands discreetly hiding a morning yawn. This was not what they'd come to hear, at least not from Laura Nostrum. After her talk there was a scattering of polite applause and already the next speaker was being announced. Pierre Zele met her on the way out. 'Miss Nostrum, that was an interesting talk but not the speech we expected.'

'I decided to change the subject,' she told him.

'Has your agency shifted its priority to Africa?' he asked, with a shade of emphasis on the word agency.

'Osage Investments has several priorities.'

She continued on her way, walking around the corner to the wooded botanical gardens across the street from her hotel. Seated near

69

the statue of the Duke of Wellington, she smoked a cigarette and watched the spray from a nearby fountain. A blonde woman about her own age was strolling nearby, carrying a black tote bag that might have contained a laptop computer. Linda ground out her cigarette and started walking again, west toward the bay. When she reached Rosia Road she turned south, heading for the harbour and dock area. She reached a building called Jumper's Bastion and paused as the blonde woman came up to her.

'Are you thinking of jumping?' she asked Linda.

'What? You startled me!'

'It's not an invitation to suicides. It was named after Captain Jumper, the first British officer to land on Gibraltar.'

'Interesting,' Linda said, avoiding the woman's eyes.

'This is one of the best harbours around.' Her casual tone suddenly disappeared and she asked, 'Who are you?'

'What?' Linda pointed to the badge still pinned to her jacket. 'Laura Nostrum.'

The woman shook her head, almost sadly. 'No, you're not. I'm Laura Nostrum. I believe your name is Linda O'Toole, since that was the only ID badge left unclaimed this morning.'

'Maybe I picked up the wrong one.'

'Maybe you did. Are you a reporter?'

Linda almost laughed at the idea. 'No, I'm

representing Osage Investments. We're trying to funnel investment money into Africa to help the economy there.'

'What made you think you could use my identity?' She sighed and tried to explain. 'I saw on the convention schedule that you were speaking this morning in a prime time slot. That reporter Fitzhugh asked if I was Laura Nostrum and I just said yes. When he mentioned the CIA connection and I saw your ID badge was unclaimed I figured you'd cancelled because of the press. So I just said I was you and spoke in your place.'

Laura Nostrum studied her with steely eyes. 'Your explanation is hard to accept. You told that reporter you were me before he mentioned the CIA. Why would you do that unless you were already planning to impersonate me?'

'I saw the item on the Internet too. The reporter's mistake gave me an opportunity to switch identities.'

'You felt safer being mistaken for a CIA agent than being plain Linda O'Toole?' When Linda didn't answer she continued, 'That reporter, Liam Fitzhugh, was murdered early this morning, stabbed to death in the Gardens across from our hotel.'

'Oh no!'

'Yes. And the police seem to think Laura Nostrum might have killed him for spreading the news of her identity.'

71

It was true. Fitzhugh had left the casino when it closed at four a.m. and someone had stabbed him along the Europa Road near the gardens. His wallet was untouched. As she listened to Nostrum relate the events, Linda felt a stab of fear not unlike the blade that must have ended Fitzhugh's life. 'Did you kill him?' she asked.

'I had nothing to do with his death. I represent an international on-line casino company. That's all you need to know. The only reason I contacted you at all was to warn you. If people believe you're me, your life could be in danger.'

'Why is the CIA interested in casinos anyway?' Linda wanted to know. 'Is this some American scheme to balance the budget?'

Linda Nostrum was not amused. She glanced around and motioned toward a nearby café with sidewalk tables. 'Let's have a drink and we'll talk some more.'

They ordered a couple of Tuskers, an African beer whose popularity had spread across the Strait, and Nostrum leaned her tote bag against the table leg between them. It was Linda's first chance to study the other woman and she saw a slender frame with an attractive face and blonde hair pulled back and knotted behind her head. She was a bit taller than

Linda, and her face was dead serious as she spoke. 'First of all, forget about the CIA. If I did have a connection with them I couldn't reveal it.'

'All right.'

'Just what did Liam Fitzhugh say to you?'

'He asked if my name was Laura Nostrum. I suppose we're about the same age and coloring. I saw my opportunity and said yes. Then he mentioned something on the Internet about my being with the CIA. I wasn't the one he wanted so I just denied it and walked on.'

'But you picked up my ID badge. Do you have any idea what this is all about?'

'No,' Linda admitted.

The woman opposite lowered her voice, though there was no one close enough to overhear their conversation. 'Do you realize how much money is skimmed off the top of casino profits each year? There was a time decades ago when the money from Las Vegas helped support organized crime. Today, with so many nations involved, it's difficult to determine where some of those casino profits go. I planned to address the issue in my talk, to warn that some of it might be funnelled to terrorist organizations.'

'Then maybe I did some good suggesting it go to the African—' She stopped suddenly as a Gibraltar Police car pulled up at the curb.

Two officers got out and the driver asked, 'Are you Laura Nostrum?'

Both women exchanged glances and the real Laura Nostrum stood up. 'That's me. What can I do for you?'

'We'd like you to accompany us to the station,' he told her. 'It's concerning the death of Mr. Liam Fitzhugh.'

'I know nothing about that.'

'We only wish to question you and take a statement.'

'Very well.' She glanced back at Linda, as if to convey some message. Then she climbed into the back seat of the patrol car with one of the officers.

Linda watched the car disappear down Rosia Road. It was only then that she realized the black tote bag still rested against the leg of their table. She picked it up and started back to the hotel. When she reached the lobby she knew the news of the reporter's killing was spreading. It was the German Spaniard from the casino who intercepted her on the way to the elevator.

'Miss Nostrum, are you all right? We heard that the reporter Fitzhugh was killed in the gardens. They say it was because he revealed your identity.'

'I—that's not true. You see, I'm not Miss Nostrum. It was all a terrible mistake.'

Bert Stein frowned at her words. 'What do you mean?'

'My name is Linda O'Toole. The police have picked up the real Laura Nostrum for

74

questioning.'

'That is bad. The police do not like interference from the CIA.'

'They're British police, not Spaniards,' she reminded him.

He shrugged. 'Police are police. Be careful, Miss O'Toole, if that is your name.'

As she made her way to her room she knew what she must do next.

*   *   *

Once in the safety of her room she opened the tote bag, revealing the laptop computer she'd expected. But when she raised the lid there was a surprise, a sticker that read: Property of the London Daily Mail. It was the dead man's computer. She took a deep breath, wondering if Laura had killed him for it. She scrolled down the e-mail list of sent items and opened the last message, addressed to someone at the paper, most likely his editor. Skimming down the screen she saw Nostrum's name and read: *Nostrum was observed speaking with a man I suspect is channelling casino profits to terrorist organizations. I am keeping an eye on the Rock.*

She stared at the screen, trying to understand the words. At the time Liam Fitzhugh sent this e-mail, he still believed she was Laura Nostrum, the purported CIA agent. And she'd noticed him nearby once or twice when she was speaking with someone. But what men had she spoken with prior to his murder? She made a quick list in her head and came up with only three: Pierre Zele, the conference organizer, the Irishman Mike Patrick, and Bert Stein from Spain. Patrick had offered to show her the rock apes and take the cable car to the Rock's observation deck. Was that why Fitzhugh had wanted to keep an eye on it?

When there was still no word that Laura Nostrum had been freed by the police, she sought out Pierre Zele and asked if he'd heard anything. 'Only that they're holding her,' he said, standing outside the theatre where a film on casinos in the Far East was being shown to delegates. 'It's best not to ask too many questions.'

'But she was on your program as a speaker!'

His eyebrows rose a fraction. 'You're forgetting, Miss Nostrum did speak to us, just this morning.'

'I . . . I shouldn't have used her name. I thought I was doing it for a good cause.'

'You're still wearing her badge.'

'She must have mine. When I see her we'll have to exchange them. I'm Linda O'Toole.'

'I see.'

She hurried away, regretting that she'd approached him at all. Back at the hotel casino, Mike Patrick caught up with her. At that moment, despite her suspicions, his friendly face was a relief. 'How about that trip to see the rock apes?'

She hesitated only a moment. 'Why not?'

'I've got a rental car. We can drive through. It's the best way to see them. They climb all over the cars.'

'Sounds exciting,' she replied with only a touch of irony.

The car was an older model that looked as if it had visited ape country before. As they started up the road toward Queen's Gate, Mike Patrick remarked casually, 'The word around the conference is that you're not Laura Nostrum at all.'

She laughed. 'There was a bit of a mix-up. I'm just a poor Irish girl named Linda O'Toole.'

'I thought you were American.'

'I am, but I work at my firm's Paris office now.'

'And they are . . . ?'

'Osage Investments.'

He grunted. Ahead of them she saw the Apes' Den, and an officer stopped them with a few words of warning. 'Stay inside the vehicle at all times and do not touch the apes. They do like to bite people. We're not responsible for injuries to yourself or your vehicle.'

They continued down the road, watching the hillside for movement. 'There's one!' Linda exclaimed, pointing to a tailless monkey about two feet tall that had suddenly come running down from the trees.

Within minutes there were three Barbary Macaques on the car, one of them effectively blocking Mike's view through the windshield. He kept driving slowly. 'They want food, I suppose. Here's a bag of berries. Throw them a few, but don't let them bite you.'

She opened the window far enough to toss some berries, and by that time two more cars had appeared behind them. One of the Macaques grabbed a berry while the other two jumped off, heading for the new arrivals. 'This is a popular place,' Linda said.

'In the busy season they have a thousand visitors a day here.'

'I can tell this isn't your first trip.'

He increased their speed as more apes headed for the car. 'I was here once before, a couple of years back.'

By then it was late afternoon, but Mike insisted they must take the cable car to the observation platform on the Rock. When they reached it, crowded in among some French and Spanish tourists, Linda had to admit it was a magnificent sight. 'Is that Africa over there?' she asked.

'It certainly is. Those are the Rif Mountains you're looking at. It's Morocco, the country of Tangier, Marrakesh, Casablanca and a thousand intrigues, only a few of them captured in the cinema. We could take the ferry across tomorrow if you have time.'

She gave her familiar laugh. 'There are enough intrigues right here on Gibraltar. This has been pleasant but I'd better be getting back. I'm anxious to learn if the police have released Miss Nostrum.'

*   *   *

Bert Stein was the first person she saw in the hotel lobby. It was he who told her the news. 'The police have released that woman, Laura Nostrum. The word is there was pressure from Washington and the Prime Minister ordered it. If the Spanish were in control it wouldn't be like that.'

'Is she back here?'

Stein shook his head. 'Zele says they're flying her to London on the first available plane.'

She glanced at her watch, wondering about the schedule. Gibraltar's airfield was at the north end of the peninsula, almost to the Spanish neutral zone, but it was barely more that two miles from the hotel. She hurried up to her room to get the laptop and then went out to the street where a few taxis were waiting. The airfield, jutting into the bay to allow the necessary length for takeoffs and landings, was located just beyond Gibraltar's sports stadium. She was there within minutes, just as the setting sun was dipping into the bay, and she only hoped it wasn't too late. A

Gibraltar police car was parked in front of the terminal, which was a good sign.

'When's the next London flight?' she asked the ticket seller.

'British Airways has a delayed flight to Gatwick boarding in twenty minutes.'

'I have to see someone waiting to board.'

The young woman stared at her. 'You can't pass through security without a boarding pass.'

Linda turned to see Laura Nostrum being escorted through security by a police officer. 'Laura!' she called out. 'Wait up!'

The blonde woman turned and recognized her at once. She shook off the officer's arm and came forward to meet her. 'What are you doing here?' she asked.

'I thought you'd want this laptop. Can I speak with you in private before you take off?'

'I only have fifteen minutes.' She glanced at the officer. 'The police are convinced I killed Fitzhugh because he blew my cover. If they see that computer they'll be sure of it. They only released me on condition that I leave Gibraltar at once.'

Linda glanced around. 'Do they have a private office we could use?'

'This is as private as it gets. Who are you, anyway?'

Linda took a deep breath. It was time for the truth. 'Interpol. I'm stationed at their Paris headquarters. We're both after the same person, the one who's diverting casino profits to terrorists. I think I know who it is, but I need you to confirm it. Washington wouldn't have sent you here unless they were suspicious of someone at the conference.'

'I'm sorry. I can't tell you a thing.'

Linda was aware that someone else had entered the terminal building behind her, but she ignored it until she saw the startled expression on Laura's face. 'He's got a gun!'

There were two shots close together as Laura pushed her to the floor. Then she realized the police officer had fired back. 'Stay down!' the officer warned them as he made his way carefully to the wounded man. Already the ticket agent was calling for help on her phone.

Their assailant was still alive, but bleeding badly. 'Who is this man?' Laura Nostrum asked as they ignored the officer and got to their feet.

'He's the one we were both looking for,' Linda told her, 'and I'm pretty sure he's Liam Fitzhugh's killer. His name is Bert Stein.'

*   *   *

The flight to London departed without Laura Nostrum. There were police reports to be filled out, and a trip back to the station for them both. The investigating detective was Lieutenant Collins and he let them know that Stein would probably live. 'He might even be

81

willing to implicate others in his skimming operation, if we're lucky. I assume that's the goal of both Interpol and the CIA. Now suppose you tell me about Fitzhugh's computer, Miss O'Toole.'

'Laura left it by our table when the police took her in for questioning this morning, obviously because if you found it in her possession you'd think she killed the reporter to obtain it.'

Collins nodded. 'We certainly would have. How did it come into your possession, Miss Nostrum?'

She shrugged. 'As soon as I heard he'd been killed I went to his room, found it and removed it.'

'Did you have a key?'

'Not an official one.'

Lieutenant Collins grunted. 'We'll let that pass.' He turned back to Linda. 'Go on, Miss O'Toole.'

'I read Fitzhugh's last e-mail to his London paper. He said he'd observed Nostrum—the name I was using at the time—speaking with the man he suspected of aiding the terrorists. I'd only spoken to three men since I arrived—Pierre Zele, Mike Patrick and Bert Stein. Fitzhugh went on to say he'd be keeping a close eye on the Rock. Did he mean the Rock of Gibraltar? Hardly! Since he was already on the Rock, how could he help but keep an eye on it? His sentence meant something else. He

82

was keeping a close eye on one of those three men, and his murder confirmed it. He must have followed one of them into the Gardens and got stabbed for his trouble. This evening after he told me Laura was on her way to London, Stein saw me come down from my room with a computer tote and hail a taxi. He didn't know what was on it, but he had to retrieve it or kill us trying.'

'I see. And how did that message tell you it was Bert Stein?'

Linda smiled when she saw by Laura's expression that she'd realized the obvious answer herself. 'Well, the names Zele and Patrick have no connection with Gibraltar, but I suddenly remembered that Stein is the German word for rock.'

Other People

Bill Kirton

A neighbour of mine, Stan, is depressed. He's sixty-four years old, tall, with plenty of white hair and a flattish stomach. He's a fit guy, plays lots of golf, still goes jogging. Three weeks ago, he got on a bus and a young woman, early thirties he thought, offered him her seat. He smiled at her, said no thanks, and he's been depressed ever since.

'I mean, it was nice of her,' he said, when he told me about it. 'Not enough politeness about, so it's good to see it.'

'So why's it depressing?' I asked.

'Because I fancied her,' he said.

'Eh?'

'Aye, there's me fantasising about getting into bed with her and all she sees is an old man.'

This story's not about Stan, but that experience of his sort of sums it up really.

It was a few years back, before the suicide bombers and all that. You might remember it. Aberdeen. Three isolated little explosions. Two killed in the worst one, one in each of the others. Then the fourth one, the last one, in the house at the end of the cul-de-sac. It was my case. CID. None of the explosions was big enough to be a terrorist thing. Although you never know, do you?

They all happened in the same area—all except the one in the house. With the first one, all hell was let loose. There wasn't a panic exactly, but it was close. With the oil companies and some Americans still here, we'd always thought we might be targeted at some stage, but it didn't look anything like that. For a start, it happened in a street in one of the . . . let's say less respectable parts of town. No multinationals there, no police stations or army posts. Just crappy, run-down houses and flats. A few immigrants, but just families. Hard to see them as shoe bombers or fanatics. It's an area that keeps us busy— muggings, burglaries, punch-ups, even a couple of murders, but not terrorism. You need belief for that stuff, and there's not much belief in anything around there.

It was just the one guy killed. Local guy, Billy Watts. He had a few convictions—GBH, drunk and disorderly, aggravated theft. Par for the course. We didn't think he was into explosives, though. People living in the street heard a bang—not a very loud one even— looked out, and there he was, dead.

We had all sorts crawling all over the place for a while. This was before the Al-Qaeda stuff, remember, so no national alerts or anything, but the anti-terrorist crews gave it the once-over. Soon lost interest. The

85

explosion was too small. (Tell that to Billy, I thought.) They put together bits and pieces, decided it was a pretty amateur, home-made thing. They reckoned he might've just been carrying a small charge to blow a safe or a lock somewhere. We kept looking, but the pressure was off.

Then the other two happened, and we got a bit twitchy. It was the same again—small explosions, amateur devices, and the guys who were killed were in the same league as Billy. First, Brian McPhee, then Jez Crainey and Joey Gallacher together. Waste of space, all of them. Needed taking off the streets. Basically, somebody was doing our job for us.

But that's not the way it looked, of course. There was something eerie about it, what with it being so small scale and personal. The major things—the bus and tube bombs—they're vile, but they're aimed at . . . well, society. A sort of abstract target. In a way—a stupid, inexcusable way—you can understand them. Sure, the victims are individuals, with families and intricate, significant little lives, but they're not the real targets. It's bizarre—the bombers are using physical things which destroy material places and persons, but they're detonated by faith and the thing they really want to destroy is an idea. Still, I suppose if your notion of heaven is a place where you get access to a few virgins, the dividing line between material and abstract's bound to be a bit vague.

Anyway, as I said, it all got a bit twitchy for a while. There was no doubt that the explosions were all linked. For a start, there was the fact that they all happened in the same area and the victims were all active members of the local underclass. But we had harder evidence than that. Our forensic guys found identical materials at each scene—same sort of explosives, same bits of packaging, clear plastic and some black, shiny stuff. Either Billy, Brian, Jez and Joey had been to the same night-school class on bombs or they'd all got their explosives from the same source.

But what the hell were they all doing with explosives anyway? It wasn't their style. The weapons they used were in their pockets or on the ends of their arms and legs. So what was going on? Gang stuff? Unlikely. Vigilantes? Possible. Hard to know where to start looking, though. We didn't have much CCTV footage to work with. Most of the cameras in the area are vandalised as soon as they're set up. In fact, there was just the one sequence, a pretty graphic one, too. It shows Brian McPhee running along. He's carrying some sort of dark-coloured bag and he's in a hurry. Then, there's a flash and he's lying on the pavement, dead. Nobody else in sight. The IT guys sharpened up the images as best they could, analysed the frames, reckoned the flash started from the bag.

We interviewed all their pals. Bit shell-shocked, some of them, so they were willing to talk for a change. Nobody thought the four dead guys were linked in any way, except Jez and Joey, who always hung out together. They all swore blind that none of them had ever had anything to do with explosives. When he was a kid, Jez used to like tying bangers to cats and dogs, but he hadn't done that for years. No, it wasn't until the explosion in the house that we began to make sense of it.

It was one of those little self-contained communities off Great Western Road. Neat granite bungalows ranged round a central area of grass and trees. Respectable folk settled in the security of the city's West End. Chalk and cheese compared with the place we've been talking about. Mrs Seaton in number 16 heard a bang one evening. Thought it was maybe just loud enough to be a gas explosion or something but, when she looked out, couldn't see anything wrong. A bit later, though, she saw smoke coming out of Mr Dunstan's house, the one at the end of the cul-de-sac, and phoned the fire brigade. They found a small fire in one of the bedrooms at the back, clear evidence of an explosion, and Mr Dunstan with a big hole in his chest and stomach.

We sent round a SOCO with his team and I got there just as he was finishing up. I didn't need him to tell me what had happened. The blast had scarred and stained the walls at waist height and made a helluva mess of Mr

Dunstan. He'd caught it full on. On the floor there were bits of bags and other containers and lots of garden fertiliser, bleach, stuff like that. I'm no expert but I knew right away what they were for.

'Here's your bomber, Jack,' said Rob Angus, the SOCO.

'Maybe,' I said. 'Who'd've thought it, eh? A bomb factory in the West End.'

Rob waved a hand at the debris.

'Hardly a factory,' he said. 'Couldn't make many out of the stuff that's here.'

'One's enough,' I said.

I looked round the rest of the house. Living room and dining room at the front, kitchen and bathroom in the middle, and the two bedrooms at the back. All muted colours, not many ornaments, no pictures on the walls. Everywhere, except the blast room, neater than I can ever manage to get my place. A model of ordinariness. I called the station to get the I.T. boys to check out his computer. It was on the table in the dining room. Bulging with lurid secrets, maybe. Nothing else was. Well, not until we started doing the basic checks on the man. That's when it got tricky.

Richard Dunstan was in his early fifties. He lived on his own and worked for a company which specialises in corporate communications. He'd bought the house three years before and, at first, that's all we could find out. Nobody knew where he'd lived previously, what his background was, anything. There was no mortgage on the house, he'd paid the full price up front. By cheque. We talked to the bank but he'd only been with them for four years, opening his accounts with small amounts and depositing big lump sums every month for the first year. He'd built up a hefty balance, used most of it to buy his house and, since then, there'd been a regular monthly cheque and plenty of other payments, all from the company he worked for. Nothing had come from any other bank, so we couldn't see back past those five years.

His postman said he thought there was 'something funny' about him because he never got any private mail. There were just the usual things from the Council and other official envelopes. There wasn't even much junk mail, except for general stuff addressed 'to the householder' and leaflets for pizza places and Chinese takeaways.

All we knew about him really was that he was definitely into making bombs and that he was the source of the ones that had killed Billy and the rest. His computer was full of material he'd downloaded about explosives and detonators. In a cupboard in the hallway, there were more bomb-making ingredients and small, Tupperware-type containers made of a plastic that matched fragments we'd found at the three locations. And, in his bedroom, he had seven identical women's handbags. Again, they were made of the shiny black material we'd found at the scene of the three explosions. Another thing that made no sense at the time—a woman's black coat hanging in a wardrobe beside his suits and jackets; nothing special, just a plain, black coat. He'd made no attempt to hide any of it, and the computer files came up as soon as our guys logged on. Either he was confident we'd never catch him, or he didn't care.

The firm he worked for was in Huntly Street. I went along with Jim Ross, my sergeant, to see if we could put some substance to the guy. We did, but it didn't get us much further. For a start, we discovered that he was self-employed and sub-contracted himself to them. So they couldn't help us with his National Insurance number or tax references.

His job was to look through the briefs sent in by potential clients, pick out any messages that might be relevant to expanding or improving their corporate communications strategy, and structure it ready for the copywriters to turn it into spin and slogans which would dazzle the market place.

'He was bloody good at it,' said the boss. 'Could think on his feet, talk the talk and walk the walk.'

(This was a communications strategist talking, remember. I was amazed the firm hadn't gone bankrupt.)

'Experienced, was he?' I asked.

'Must've been,' he said.

'What about his CV, references?'

A smile crept into his face.

'He was different. They broke the mould with him. Not like anybody else I've met in the business.'

'How?'

'Hard to say. One of a kind. Strange habits.'

'What d'you mean?'

He just shrugged. I was wishing he'd put less effort into his smile and more into his thinking.

'It would really help us,' I said, 'if you could maybe give us an example. Anything.'

The smile notched down to maybe 500 watts. Then he gave a sort of choked laugh.

'OK. When he first came here, right? The first three, four weeks. He never left his desk. No lunch, no coffee breaks, he never even went for a pee.'

Jim and I looked at each other.

'How d'you know?' I asked. 'Do you keep the key to the lavvy?'

He laughed louder, as if I was Tommy Cooper.

'About his references, though, his CV . . . '

'Well, he had the references, alright, but no CV.'

'Why not?'

'He sent in a DVD presentation. Sold

himself. Bloody clever. We used some of it in one of our campaigns. Turned out to be a win-win situation for all of us.'

'Taking a chance, weren't you?' I said. 'Not knowing his background.'

The smile didn't fade.

'We interviewed him and he hit us with another presentation, completely different, right out of left field. We had to get him on board.'

'You didn't check the references?'

The choked laugh again.

'What's the point? If you give me a referee, it's not going to be somebody who'll say you're a prick, is it? Waste of time.'

'Have you still got their names? We'd like to check them out.'

'Sure. I'll get Maureen to look them out for you.'

His smile was beginning to get to me. We were talking about an employee who'd blown himself up (after killing four other people), and yet the guy was responding as if it were a minor PR problem. I think Jim could sense my irritation because he took over and started asking about the sort of work Dunstan did for them.

'If he's as good as you say, how come he was happy to stay with you? He must've had other offers,' he said.

'No idea,' said Smiley. 'He just didn't seem to have any ambition. No va-va-voom. Great ideas, but that seemed to be enough. Whatever you gave him, he just did it and moved on. With Richard, what you saw was what you got. He should've been an academic.'

'Why?'

'Well, sitting in a room, playing around with words. Academics, isn't it?'

(So much for higher education.)

'So you're saying that all this . . . brilliance of his—it was just a job,' I said.

The smile dropped away as he thought about it.

'No. There was more to him than that. I think he did get a buzz when something worked. He liked seeing his stuff in clients' brochures and presentations. Got a little kick out of it. But then he just got on with the next job. Liked to win the battles, but didn't care about the war.'

The smile came back. He was pleased with the image.

After more of the same from him, we went into the main office and talked with some of the others there. All except two of them were a bit more subdued, a bit more aware of how serious it was. The two exceptions wore their own versions of the boss's grin and one of them practised his golf grip on a ruler as he talked to us. We asked him about Dunstan not leaving his desk, even for a pee. His smile regressed, became a smirk. He held up his hand and crooked his little finger.

'His name,' he said. 'Richard, right? Dick.'

He wiggled the finger. I wondered what his specialisation in communications strategy was. Wit, maybe.

'So you think he stayed away from the lavatory because he had a small willie?' I said.

He laughed, stretched his hand towards me and wiggled the finger again.

'Hilarious,' I said.

He changed the angle of his hand, made his forefinger into a gun and did the shooting gesture at me. Maybe he was the office Marcel Marceau. We left him before he started his invisible wall routine.

Sitting at a terminal in a side office away from the rest was a young woman called Sally. She was one of the serious ones. Really tried to help us. The trouble was, she had strange eyes. You know, the opposite to cross-eyed, one of them looking just slightly outwards. Hard to say which one. They made it difficult for me to concentrate on what she was saying. She was shocked by what had happened to Dunstan but, when we asked what she thought of him, she didn't let it affect her answer.

'He was hard,' she said.

'Really? How?' asked Jim.

She shrugged.

'I don't know. Hard. If he got an idea in his head, he wouldn't give in. There was no compromising.'

'Was he difficult to work with, then?'

She nodded and looked directly at me. Or rather, her left eye did. I wondered if the right one was looking at Jim.

'Sometimes. If you criticised his ideas, he got defensive. Insecure, I suppose. He'd change, go all cold. Not talk to you for a couple of days.'

'Sounds a bit childish,' I said.

She looked at me, I think.

'No,' she said. 'Insecure. Strange guy. It was as if you weren't just discussing his ideas but actually challenging him, having a go at him. Then he'd be all . . . in your face. He was worse with the men.'

'In what way?'

'Well, some of the comments he made. Cruel, really. He'd see a weakness and be in there, sharp as a knife.'

'And he didn't care if he upset them?'

'Not really. He enjoyed it. It was the same as with work. When he put together something he knew was good, you could tell. There was . . . I don't know . . . a smugness about him. It was the same when he was putting somebody down. Maybe he was just competitive.'

'But just with the men?'

'Mostly, yes. He was more . . . gentle with us.'

'Did you ever socialise with him? Drinks after work, that sort of thing?' I asked.

'No. Some of us meet up sometimes, but never Richard. He never came to any of the

96

office parties or anything. I think he had secrets. Not just the bombs, other things.'

'What sort of things?'

'I don't know. I think something bad must have happened to him. You could sort of sense it. Sometimes, he'd . . . just go quiet. And you could see . . . I don't know, things in his face.'

She was really trying to help but, to my disgust, half the time I was just studying her eyes, wondering whether she saw things differently. In fact, the more I looked at them, the more attractive they got. Bloody testosterone again.

'D'you know if he had a girl-friend?' I asked, trying to remember how to be professional.

'Don't think so. He never talked about one.'

'Your boss seems to think he was . . . unusual?' I said.

She nodded.

'He was.'

She frowned. It threw shadows into her eyes. I was beginning to obsess about them.

'A few times, he came in with bruises on his face,' she said. 'Once, he had a big piece of sticking plaster on his forehead. Right across.'

'Did he say how he'd got it?'

'No. "Accident", that's all he said. It was like nothing had happened.'

'How long ago was that?'

Again, the shrug.

'Can't remember. It was just . . . strange. I mean, the rest of the time he was just . . . well, him. Not exactly macho man. Hard to think of him in a fight.'

'That's what it was, was it? A fight?'

'Certainly looked like it.'

We didn't get much more out of her and, reluctantly, I said goodbye to her eyes. Jim said he hadn't noticed them. He's married though. Has to pretend he doesn't look at other women.

The only other thing we got was the information about Dunstan's referees from Maureen. A GP and a university professor. And guess what. When we check them out, we find they're both dead. Nothing suspicious. They'd both died around the same time, four years before, and there'd been notices about them in the paper. Little obituaries. We checked the GP's surgery and the university and, surprise, surprise, there was nothing linking them with Dunstan.

So, we've got a clever bugger with no past who's competitive but not ambitious, defensive but helpful, hard and soft, cruel and gentle. He's carrying some dark secret, and he walks into doors every so often.

When we talked to his neighbours, it got even worse.

Mrs Seaton, the one who'd phoned in about the fire, was very upset about it all. Not just because of having a bomb maker near her house, but because she thought he was such a nice man. She's in her eighties and, apparently, he'd shown her nothing but kindness. Every time he mowed his own lawn, he'd bring his mower along and do hers, too.

'He even used to do all the edges,' she said.

I looked out at her garden. It was all little islands of flowers, paved paths winding amongst them. There were edges everywhere. Cutting that lot really was neighbourly.

'I can be a fussy old witch,' she went on. 'But he always smiled, always had a little joke. And he'd always get exactly what I put on the list.'

'The list?' I said.

'The shopping list.'

'So he did your shopping?'

'Yes, he was always asking if I needed anything. And if I did, he'd get it. And he always got it right. Right amounts, right sorts. He was a gentleman. I used to tell him he'd make somebody a fine husband.'

'What did he say?'

She smiled and put her hand to her mouth, a strange, little girl sort of gesture.

'Said why did he need a wife when he had me.' She paused, then added, 'I said he could be my toy-boy.'

It's ageist, I know, but the thought was so repulsive that I found it hard to return her smile.

'What about friends?' I said. 'Did he have any visitors?'

Her answer was immediate. She obviously spent a lot of her time watching what went on

99

in the street.

'Only the one.'

'Oh?'

'Yes. A lady. I think it must have been his mother, or auntie or something. She wasn't as old as me but she wasn't young either. Had the start of osteoporosis, by the look of her. You know, stooped over.'

'Was she a regular?'

'No. I only saw her maybe four or five times. Used to see her leave in the evening. She must have stayed with him as well, though.'

'Why?'

'Well, one night she arrived very late. It was after the ten o'clock news.'

'Did you ever mention her to Mr Dunstan?'

She looked down at her hands, all crevices and folds.

'No. I didn't like to. None of my business. I saw her at the bus stop once. I said hello but I don't think she heard me.'

'And there was nobody else?'

'Not that I saw,' she said.

Mrs Seaton would have gone on talking to us for hours but we didn't need to hear about Mrs Beattie's son in Finland, or how Mr Fraser and his wife were separated but still had dinner together every night, or that the new minister at the church made inappropriate jokes in his sermons. We moved on to her neighbour, Mr Arnold. He said we could call him Baz. We didn't.

He was late thirties, a bit flash. The colour of his shirt was painful to the eyes. When we asked him about Dunstan's visitor, he confirmed what I'd suspected about Mrs Seaton.

'If I want to know anything about anybody in a quarter mile radius, Lizzie's the one I go to. If she only saw the one visitor, that's all he had.'

'But you never saw her yourself.'

'No. I'm out all day. Never back before seven.'

'So you never saw much of Mr Dunstan either, then.'

He shook his head, put up his hand and pulled at the little gelled peaks of his hair.

'Now and then. Weekends sometimes. Not often.'

'Did it surprise you when you heard what he was doing in his house?' asked Jim.

'Bloody hell, what do you think? The quiet little poof down the road turns out to be a terrorist?'

'Is that what he was, then?'

'What, a poof? I think so, yeah. Probably gay.'

He threw the remark away, as if it wasn't important.

'Why d'you say that?' I asked.

Both his hands were now playing with his peaks. He was sitting well back in his chair, relaxed, unconcerned that we were discussing a bomb maker.

'Well, you can tell, can't you? No interest in football. Never down the pub. I don't know, just the look of him. The way he was. Sort of effeminate. Girlie sort of walk.' He suddenly brought his hands back down and sat forward. 'Don't get me wrong. I've got nothing against them. They give me the creeps, though.'

Where Mrs Seaton had been willing to talk all night, 'Baz' quickly started showing little signs of impatience as we asked more questions. He didn't have much more to offer anyway so I grabbed the chance to get away from his shirt.

The rest of the people in the street confirmed that Dunstan had mostly kept himself to himself, smiled, said hello, and generally been a good enough neighbour. Only one of them injected a little sourness. She was Mrs Gordon, a young mother with two small daughters. She lived in number 26, four houses away from Dunstan's.

'Well, nowadays, you worry, don't you?' she said.

'What about?' I asked.

She pointed through the window at her kids. They were playing on her front lawn with some big rubber thing. They were maybe six and eight, something like that.

'Children,' she said. 'The things you hear, see on the telly. You can't take your eyes off them.'

She was deliberately speaking in broad terms, unwilling to be more specific. But she was the one who'd made the connection.

'And what's that got to do with Mr Dunstan?' I asked.

'Well . . . you worry, don't you? He was . . . He seemed . . . interested in Jill and Gemma.'

'Interested? How?'

'Always used to . . . stop outside. Talked to them. He didn't do anything but . . . I just didn't like it. It was creepy.'

'That was all? He just talked to them?'

'I know. It sounds as if I'm being paranoid. But you worry. You just do.'

In some ways, our final call was the strangest of the lot. At number 32, we rang the bell and the door was opened by a woman wearing the full Muslim gear. Not the burka, with the panel in the hood—the other one, the niqab I think it's called. Long black dress, black scarf on her head and black veil right up to her eyes. In fact, we couldn't see her eyes either because she was wearing tinted glasses. It was a bit of a shock because, even though you see plenty of women in headscarves nowadays, I'd never seen one in the full kit in Aberdeen before. And the only reason I mention her is not for anything she had to say—most of her answers were monosyllabic and she obviously knew nothing at all about Dunstan—but for the strangeness of our chat. You see, I've absolutely no idea who was inside all that

103

black material. Could've been a man for all I knew. There was no body language, no facial expressions, not even a look in her eyes to go on. I don't know whether our questions offended her, whether she resented being asked them, whether she thought we were accusing her of something. There was no way of gauging her reactions.

Jim said the same thing and agreed that it was . . . well, disconcerting. I mean, you need to assess people, need to know what tone to take with them, how best to get their trust, let them know your intentions. I'm not saying she shouldn't wear it—she's got every right to, if that's what she believes—but I wonder whether she knows how difficult it makes things. Muslims are getting such a bad deal nowadays that I'd hate to think I said something that offended her, but there was no way I could tell.

'Mind you,' said Jim, 'Dunstan didn't wear any of that clobber but we're just as much in the dark about him.'

'Yep,' I said. 'All that stuff from work, and now he's a good neighbour, a poof and a paedophile, too.'

'Busy guy.'

'Yes. Natural enough, though. I mean, if your hobby's blowing folk up, you're bound to seem a bit strange.'

Jim nodded but, as I spoke, I couldn't help feeling that there was something else. OK, part of the deal with bombers is that they have to put up screens. Wouldn't make much sense to wander about in Osama Bin Laden gear, muttering curses in Arabic and calling folk infidels. The screens they use are the ultra-normal ones. Nice, quiet lad. Good neighbour. Wouldn't say boo to a goose. That sort of thing. They don't want to do anything to attract attention. But Dunstan was the opposite. Everybody, especially the folk in his office, had him tagged as a weirdo. There was something else about him. Something we were missing.

Back at the station, we talked through it all and it was obvious that we had plenty of interesting opinions, but that we were a bit light on facts. Why would Dunstan become a bomber? And who the hell was he? Where was he from? How could he suddenly just appear?

We decided to concentrate on his background. Leave the abstract stuff about personality aside and find the official identity, the one made of material stuff, like bank accounts, NI number, mortgage payments, credit cards, passports, driving licences, that sort of thing. If he had suddenly 'appeared' he must have 'disappeared' from somewhere else at the same time.

Jim put as many of the squad as he could on searching through the files and archives, beginning with the time he'd opened his bank account and working back. They were looking mainly at reports of missing persons. It took them a while and we followed up a few names which led to dead ends, two family reunions and lots of embarrassing encounters with people who didn't want their families to know where they were. But with one name, we hit the jackpot. On its own, it was nothing much but, when we put it together with other pieces of evidence, it was obvious right away that we'd found him.

Dunstan had opened his account in October. In June of the same year, a journalist called Sam McManus had given in his notice, sold the entire contents of his house in Banchory, fifteen or so miles west of Aberdeen, then sold the house itself and, once everything was settled, he'd vanished.

What made him different from the others was the fact that the house had originally belonged to his mother. He'd lived there with her and inherited it when she died. It was the manner of her death which pulled all sorts of strings together.

It was no normal death. One day in March, she'd caught the bus to Aberdeen to do some shopping. CCTV picked her up in several places in and around Union Street. Then, late afternoon, at the sort of time you'd expect her to be going home, she'd got on a bus heading in the wrong direction. It was just a local, Aberdeen bus and nobody knew why she'd taken it. Maybe she was confused or maybe she was planning to visit someone. Whatever it was, she got off in King Street then, apparently, she'd wandered off into various side streets.

A 999 call came into the station just before seven. A local resident had seen her lying on a pavement, bleeding. We followed the ambulance to the hospital but she was dead before they got there. She had no handbag, no identification. There were bruises on her face, neck and head and the autopsy found that her skull had been fractured. She'd been mugged. That's how Sam McManus lost his mother, and it happened in the area where all the recent explosions had taken place.

OK, it was all circumstantial, but it was enough for us to set up some DNA tests. We still had Mrs McManus's profile, so we checked Dunstan's place, looking for samples for comparison. There were plenty—on a mug in the kitchen, in a couple of hairbrushes, a toothbrush—all sorts of things. We had to wait for them to be processed but, when the results came through, that was it. Perfect matches. No room for any doubt. Richard Dunstan was Sam McManus. And his mother's mugging gave us a pretty good motive.

But there was still more to it.

When we got the results, Jim and I went for a pint and put it all together. In the end, it made sense, it was pretty coherent.

McManus was definitely the bomb maker.

And the motive was a pretty strong one. When we asked around in Banchory, we got the same picture that we'd got with Dunstan—an odd, secretive guy with a sharp tongue who got his retaliation in first. No friends, no social life. A loner. He'd been very close to his mother. Looked after her. But then, she looked after him, too. In a strange way, they were a perfect couple. When she was killed, he disappeared even before he'd sold the house. Nobody saw him. He locked himself away. Then, of course, he vanished. And that was enough for me to think that he was already planning something. Otherwise, why go to the trouble of giving himself a new identity? OK, he wanted a break from his grief, wanted to get away from the place which had associations with his mother. But a new name? A new person? Bit extreme.

Anyway, he makes bombs. And none of them was self-detonating. The fragments of stuff the bomb lads had collected each time made them pretty sure that they'd been set off by remote control, and they'd found exactly the sort of detonators to do that in amongst the stuff at his place. They were just like little telly remotes—not very powerful, no good for long range signals. You'd need to be fairly near the bomb, but with some protection.

So the only question really was, how the hell did he plant the bombs on Billy and the others? We couldn't prove anything but it seemed to me that there were enough indicators to suggest that there was a lot of poetic justice involved. For a start, there was the old woman that Mrs Seaton had seen visiting him. She'd seen her leaving in the evenings and, once, coming back after the ten o'clock news. And, when she spoke to her at the bus stop, no reply. So who was she?

Easy. It was Dunstan.

When you think about it, everything fits. Why's he got the woman's coat in his bedroom? Why the job lot of identical handbags? He dresses up as a stooped old woman, sticks enough explosive to do just local damage in a handbag, and wanders around the area where his mother had been mugged. Easy target. Come and get me, lads. And they do. First Billy, then the others. The bruises that Sally had seen weren't from fights, they were from muggings. Dunstan gets knocked down, they grab his bag, and they're home free. Until they get round the corner and he presses the button.

Without corroboration, we couldn't prove it but I'm pretty sure that's how it happened. In the end, there was no real mystery. Only the one that we're all stuck with. Dunstan was elusive. He was all sorts of things to all sorts of people. Nobody knew him. Everybody was shocked when they heard what he'd been doing. But we're all the same. Who am I? Who are you? We like to think we know but, really, we're at the mercy of other people. They get

109

some sort of impression of us, make a quick judgement, and that's that. As far as they're concerned, that's who we are. And the person we think we are is lurking somewhere underneath all the layers, with no hope in hell of ever getting out. It's like Stan and the girl on the bus.

Mind you, Dunstan had had to work at it more than most. Sally with the eyes was right. He had a much bigger secret. As Sam McManus, he'd been hiding things long before his mother died, long before any of this stuff. It's something I didn't tell you before but it made much more sense of everything folk thought of him. And it made me wonder even more how the hell we can be who we are. Forgive the pun, but it was a little bombshell our pathologist dropped on us after the autopsy. Mrs McManus never had a son. She had just the one child. A daughter. Samantha.

Sins of Scarlet

Robert Barnard

Cardinal Pascona stood a little aside from his fellow electors, observing the scene, conjecturing on the conversations that were animating every little knot of cardinals. The elderly men predominated, of course. The young men were not only in a minority, but they were unlikely to want any of their number to be elected. A long papacy was the last thing anybody wanted at this juncture. So instead of forming up into a clique of their own, they separated and mingled with the older men. They were all, in any case, related in some way or other to earlier popes, and their opinions for that reason tended to be discounted. That was unfair but understandable.

Cardinal Borromei.

That was the name that kept coming towards him, through the sticky and fetid air of the Chapel. It was clear to Pascona that opinion was drifting—had already drifted—in that direction. Borromei was related to a previous pope, like the young men, but his promotion to the rank of cardinal at the age of twenty-three was now so long ago that everybody had discounted it. He had proved his worth to the College by a long life of steady opinions, safe hands on the tiller, and general mediocrity. He was a man to ruffle no feathers, stir up no hornet's nests, raise no high winds.

Ideal.

Or ideal in the view of most of his fellow electors. And promising in other ways too: aged sixty-seven and obese from a fondness for rich and outré foods. That, and a partiality for the finest cognac, marked him out as likely to be present before long in the Chapel in mummified form only. Cardinal Pascona stepped down from the chapel stalls and began mingling with the knots of his fellows. The conversations were going as he had expected.

'The situation in France is becoming worrying,' that old fool da Ponti was saying to a little group of like-minded ciphers. 'Borromei has been used to a mediation role in Venice. Couldn't be bettered at the present time.' He continued looking at him, and Pascona knew that any dissent would be discounted as the bile of an unsuccessful candidate. Everyone in the Conclave assessed Pascona as *papabile* but there was a distinct reluctance to vote for him.

'Absolutely,' Pascona said with a smile. 'A perfectly safe pair of hands, and accustomed to bringing peace to warring factions.' He could not restrain himself from adding: 'Though whether the Bourbons—fair-weather friends to us, at their best—deserve the services of the

Church's best mediator is another matter. The unkind might suggest that they deserve to stew in a juice of their own making.'

And he moved on, with a peaceful, delightful glide as if, having just dispensed a Christ-like wisdom, he was currently walking on air.

The bowls from their light supper were just being cleared away. Pascona nodded in the direction of the robed and cowled figures who silently served them and waited for them to bring the silver goblets with their nightcaps in them. A vile red wine from Sicily in all probability. It was generally agreed among the cardinals that everything was done to make their stay incommunicado from the real world (if Rome and the Vatican was that) as unpleasant as possible. The aim of the Vatican officials was to persuade them to make a decision as quickly as they reasonably could so that a return to normality could be achieved. After all, for those officials, it was only a matter of one old man being succeeded by another old man. Nothing much happened during the last reign, and (unless a surprising choice was made) nothing much would happen in the next one.

Cardinal Pascona took up his goblet. It was indeed a vile wine, quite incredibly sour and thick. Prolonged indigestion or worse could well be the consequences for many of the elderly and infirm electors if they did more than sip at such muck. Confident in his own stomach the Cardinal drank, then went over to another group.

'It is a sobering thought,' he injected into their small-talk that was by now a mere prelude to slumber, 'that the world is waiting on our decision, but when the choice is announced everyone will say "Who?"'

The cardinals smiled politely, though one or two of the smiles were sour. Not all of them liked to be thought totally insignificant in the wider scheme of things. Now the cowled figures were going round extinguishing the nests of candles on the walls. They rolled out the down mattresses and put on top of them a pillow and a pile of blankets hardly needed in the close atmosphere of the Sistine. Beside these bundles they put a nightlight. No great comforts for a long night. Cardinals removed their red robes and lay down in their substantial undergarments. Bones creaked as they levered themselves down. Cardinal Pascona took great care not to creak himself. He was still fit and active in every way. That ought to be noticed. He was not going to live for ever, but he had a few years yet in him, and good ones too.

He lay on his back looking up. Nothing could be seen of the ceiling, but in the murky light cast by the few remaining nightlights he could distinguish the contours of the Chapel. He had loved the Chapel since he had first seen it fifty years before. It spoke to him. Twenty years before, when he was barely forty, he had become part of a commission to report on the state of the Chapel, in particular on the state of Mazzuoli's restorations at the beginning of the century. Pascona had sat on the scaffolding day after day, eventually dressing as a workman, sharing their bread and wine, getting to *know* every inch of the ceiling and the altar wall and the Last Judgement fresco. The Commission had reported, but nothing had been done. Business as usual at the Vatican!

He altered the position of his bed so that his head was towards the altar. He did not want to think of the Last Judgement. Fine, terrifying, but the Christ was not his Christ—too commanding, too much an obvious man of action. A general, an organiser, that was Michaelangelo's Christ. Whereas his was gentler, more of a healer, more forgiving, surely?

He lay in the darkness, his eyes fixed on the panels he could not see, recreating the scenes he knew so well, that had been imprinted on his soul some twenty years before. The drunken Noah, a rare scene of comedy, and to the right of that panel his favourite of all the *ignudi*—the naked men holding medallions. A boy-man, infinitely inviting, conscious of his own appeal—delightful, inexhaustible.

But then he let his eyes sweep across the

darkness of the ceiling and fix on the central panel. The masterpiece among masterpieces in his opinion. The moment of creation. And in particular Adam: beautiful, languid before full awakening, holding hope and promise for all of Cardinal Pascona's tastes. And so like his own beloved Sandro! The yearning face, the beautiful body—it was as if Sandro had been created for him in the likeness of our first father.

He slept.

He awoke next morning to the sounds of disturbance—shouting, choking, vomiting and groans. He leapt from his bed. The Chapel was now fully illuminated and he ran to a little group of cardinals in a circle, gazing down in consternation. In the middle of the circle, writhing on the stone floor, lay the obese figure of Cardinal Borromei. Pascona could only make out one word of his cries.

'Aiudo!'

He immediately took control.

'Help he must have. Summon a doctor!'

Cardinal da Ponti stepped in with his usual statement of the obvious.

'You know we cannot allow one in. The best we can do is get him out of the Chapel to be treated there.'

'And that of course is what we must do.'

'But he should be here. Today might be the day when . . . And it might just be indigestion.'

Cardinal Pascona paused, momentarily

116

uncertain.

'Cardinal Borromei is someone who enjoys the pleasures of the table. But there have been few pleasures of the table on offer here in the Chapel. Spartan fare every day so far. The wine last night was disgraceful . . . '

He was about to put aside his indecision and insist that the tormented man be removed and treated outside the Chapel when the whole body of cardinals was transfixed by a terrible cry. The flabby body on the floor arched, shuddered, then sank motionless back to the floor.

'È morto?' someone whispered.

Dead was certainly what he seemed to be. Cardinal Pascona knelt by the body, felt his chest, then put his face and ear close to his mouth. He shook his head.

'Dead,' he said. 'We must—with the permission of the Cardinal Chamberlain—remove the body. Then we must put out a statement to the waiting crowds. I think it should specify a *colpo di sangue* as the cause of death. A stroke.'

'But it didn't look—'

Cardinal Pascona put up his hand and turned to Cardinal da Ponti.

'I specify that because it is easily understood by the least sophisticated member of the crowd. Everyone there will have had some family member—a grandfather, an uncle—who has died of a stroke. It is a question of

117

getting the message across with the least fuss. If some amendment is needed after the doctors have examined him—so be it. But I do not anticipate any need for it.'

'But a death in Conclave—and *such* a death: a man who, if I might put it so, was the *favourite.*'

Cardinal Pascona was brusque in the face of such tastelessness.

'But what could be more likely? A large number of elderly men, shut up together in an unhealthy atmosphere, on a diet which—to put it mildly—is not what they are accustomed to. And the candidate in a state of extreme excitement. It has happened before, and it is a wonder that it hasn't happened more often.'

The thought that there had been a precedent excited them all.

'Oh, *has* it happened?' asked Cardinal Morosi. Pascona ignored him. He addressed the whole College, summoned from their beds or from the *prima Colazione* by that terrible last cry.

'The need now is to remove, with all appropriate ceremonies and mourning, the deceased brother, and then to continue our deliberations. The world awaits our decision. We must not be found wanting at this crisis in our history, and that of the world.'

It struck nobody that for Cardinal Pascona 'the whole world' meant effectively the Western half of Europe. They busied

118

themselves, summoned the waiting monks who were clearing away the breakfast things, and had Cardinal Borromei removed from the Chapel. Having someone willing and able to take charge enlivened their torpid and aging intellects, and they settled down to discussions in groups with zest and vigour. What was a death, after all, to men for whom it was only a beginning?

Yet, oddly, the initiative and address of Cardinal Pascona had an effect on the discussion which was the reverse of what might have been expected. Put bluntly (which it never was in this Conclave), it might have been summed up in the phrase 'Who does he think he is?' The fact that they were all grateful to him for taking charge, were conscious that he had avoided several hours of indecision and in-fighting, did not stop them asking by what right he had taken control at that moment of crisis in the affairs of the Church.

'He takes a great deal too much on himself,' one of them said.

And it did his chances no good at all.

For though Pascona was *papabile*, he was not the only one to be so. There had been a minor stir of interest in the early days of the Conclave in favour of Cardinal Fosco, Archbishop of Palermo. He was a man who had no enemies, usually spoke sense, and was two or three years on the right side of senility. True there was one thing against him. This was

119

not the fact that he had something of an obsession about a rag-tag-and-bobtail collection of criminals in his native island. It was the Mafia this, the Mafia that the whole time, as if they were set to take over the world. That the cardinals shrugged off and suffered. But what was really against him in many cardinals' eyes was his height. He was barely five feet tall (or 1.5 metres, as the newfangled notions from France had it). Just to be seen by the crowd he would have to have several cushions on his throne when he went out on the balcony to bless the masses. It was likely to cause ridicule, and the Church was aware, since Voltaire, of how susceptible it was to wit, irony and proletarian laughter.

But suddenly, it seemed, Fosco was a decidedly desirable candidate.

Pascona watched and listened in the course of the day. Ballot succeeded ballot, with nothing so democratic as a declaration of the result. But the word went around: the vote for Fosco was inching up, that for Pascona slowly ebbing away. The Cardinal went around, talking to all and sundry with imperturbable urbanity—amiable to all, forswearing all controversy. He was among the first to collect his frugal evening meal. By then his mood was contemplative. He gazed benignly at the monks serving the *stufato*, then looked down in the direction of the Cardinal from Palermo. As he helped himself to the rough bread there was the tiniest of nods from one of the cowled heads.

'Dear Michelangelo, help one of your greatest admirers and followers,' he prayed that night on his narrow bed. 'Let the vote go to a follower of yourself, as well as a devout servant of Christ.'

Before he slept his mind went not to the *ignudi*, nor to the awakening Adam in the great central panel, but away from the altar to the expelled Adam as, with Eve, and newly conscious of sin, he began the journey out of Paradise.

He smiled, as thoughts of Sandro and their forthcoming pleasures when they were united again warmed his aging body.

The morning was not a repeat of the day before.

Over breakfast there was talk, and before long it was time to take the first test of opinion, to find out whether straw should be added to the burning voting slips to make black smoke, or whether it should be omitted, to the great joy of the crowds in St Peter's Square as the white smoke emerged. One cardinal had not risen from his bed, and he was the most important of all. Cardinal da Ponti went to shake him awake, then let out a self-suppressed gasp of dismay. The cardinals, oppressed by fear and horror, hurried over to the bed.

Cardinal Fosco lay, a scrap of humanity,

121

dead as dead. He looked as if he could be bundled up, wrapped in a newssheet, and put out with the rubbish from the Conclave's meals.

'*Dio mio!*'

The reactions were various, but more than one started to say what was on everybody's minds.

'But he too was the—'

This time they hesitated to use the term from horse-racing. But one by one, being accustomed to bow to authority, they looked towards the man who, only yesterday, had set the tone and solved the problem of what should be done. Somehow Pascona, with his long experience of curias and conclaves, knew they would do that, and was ready. He cleared his throat.

'Fellow cardinals. Friends,' he began. 'Let us pray for our friend whom God has called to himself. And let us at the same time pray for guidance.' There was a murmur of agreement, along with one or two murmurs of something else. After a minute's silence Cardinal Pascona resumed, adopting his pulpit voice.

'I believe we all know what must be done. I think God has spoken to us, each and every one, at this crisis moment—spoken as God always does speak, through the silent voice of our innermost thoughts.' The cardinals muttered agreement, though most of them had had nothing in the interval for silent prayer that could honestly be called a thought. 'He has told us that what must be thought of first at this most difficult moment is the Church: its good name, its primacy and power, and its mission to bring to God all waverers, all wrong-doers, all schismatics. It is the Church and its God-given mission that must be in the forefront of all our minds.'

There was a more confident buzz of agreement.

'We are in a crisis, as I say, in the history of ours, the one true church. In the world at large doubt, distrust and rebellion seethe, distracting the minds of the unlettered, provoking the discontent of the educated. Ridicule, distrust of long-held beliefs, rebellion against the position of the natural leaders of Society—all these evils flourish today, as never before. At such a point any event—even an innocent and natural occurrence such as we witness here—' he gestured towards the human scrap on the bed—'will be taken up, seized upon as a cause of scandal and concern, distorted and blackened with the ingenuity of the Devil himself, who foments and then leads all such discontents and rebellions. Let us make our minds up, let us make our choice quickly, let us conceal what has happened until such a time as it can be announced and accepted as the natural event which in truth it was.'

This time there was a positively enthusiastic

reception for his words.

'Come my friends,' resumed Pascona, delighted at the effect of his words, 'let us get down to business. Let us vote, and let us vote to make a decision, and to present to the world a front of unity and amity. And let us treat our friend here with the respect that a lifetime of faithful service demands. Put a blanket over him.'

It worked like a charm. A blanket was thrown over the body of the dead Cardinal Fosco, leaving his head showing. Not dead, only resting seemed to be the message. The living cardinals proceeded to a vote, and even before the last vote was in and counted it was clear that the straw would no longer be required: the smoke would be pure white.

The excitement was palpable. While they remained cloistered in the Chapel the other cardinals thumped Pascona on the shoulder and indulged in such bouts of kiddishness as were possible to a collection of men dominated by the dotards. After five minutes of this, and as the Chapel was penetrated by sounds of cheering from crowds in the Square, the new Pope proceeded to the passageway from the Chapel to St Peter's, pausing at the door to look towards the altar and the massive depiction of the Last Judgement behind it. Magnificent, but quite wrong, he thought. And perhaps a silly superstition at that.

Then he proceeded into the upper level of

the great Church, then along towards the door leading on to the balcony. He stopped before the throne, raised on poles like a sedan chair. He let the leading cardinals, led by the Cardinal Chamberlain and helped by the monks who had serviced the Conclave, robe him and bestow on him all the insignia of his new office. He behaved with impeccable graciousness.

'What name has Your Holiness decided to be known by?' asked the Chamberlain. Pascona paused before replying.

'I am conscious of the links of my mother's family to this great, this the *greatest* office. The fame of Alexander VI will live forever, but the name is too precious for me, and for the Church, for me to assume it. In truth it would be a burden. I shall leave that sacred name to my ancestor, and I shall take the name of the other Pope from her family. I shall be known as Calixtus IV.'

The Chamberlain nodded.

From the Square there came sounds. Someone, perched somewhere, with good eyesight, must have been able to see through the open door of the balcony. A whisper, then a shout, had gone round.

'It's the Borgia. The Borgia!'

The fame of his mother's family easily eclipsed that of his father's. The tone of the shouts had fear in it, but also admiration, anticipation. What a time Alexander VI's had been! Bread and circuses, and lots of sex. Calixtus IV smiled to himself, then ascended the throne. As he was about to nod to the four carriers to proceed through the door and on to the balcony, one of the monks came forward with a bag of small coins, to scatter to the crowd below. As he handed the bag to the Pope, he raised his head and the cowl slipped back an inch or two. There was the loved face: the languid eyes of Michaelangelo's Adam, the expression of newly-awakened sensuality, and underneath the coarse robe the body, every inch of which Calixtus knew so well. He took the bag, and returned his gaze.

'Grazie, Ales-*Sandro*,' he said.

Tour New Zealand in Five Easy Murders

Yvonne Eve Walus

The 3rd one, Christchurch

When I tell people I'm a criminal profiler, respectful silence falls on the conversation. I know what they're thinking: Sherlock Holmes, challenging cases, complex scientific methods.

That image is about as close to the truth as prostitution is to a glam way of spending your evenings with cocktails and distinguished gentlemen.

Speaking of prostitution, there's been another killing. That's why they called me in. I was shuffling my usual load of dusty files, with trails as cold as winter sand, when the boss stuck his head into my cubicle.

'Fuck all that, Cupcake,' he said. 'We have a live one here.'

An ironic choice of words, given the state the victim was in.

It's difficult to be a woman in this job. 'You won't have the stomach,' they'd said when I applied. What they'd meant was, I wouldn't have the imagination. Getting into the mind of a serial killer (and I'm not being sexist here when I say they're all male) is difficult enough for any so-called normal person, but for a woman to try to get inside such a man's head . . . that's next to impossible.

Up till now, the only head I'd needed to get into was my boss's when I wanted a raise—which I managed; and my ex boyfriend's—which I did not. Profiling the home invaders, the restaurant arsonists and the small-scale extortionists didn't require a lot of imagination. I would study the crime scenes (mostly from photographs) and the statistics (mostly from tedious reports), I would pore over the evidence and produce profiles good enough for positive id.

Up till now.

'That's the third one this year and it follows the pattern,' I heard moments later in the emergency meeting. 'A prostitute on her night off, a back street, a strike to the head hard enough to stun, followed by strangulation. In each case, autopsy revealed a first class dinner eaten a few hours beforehand. As to sexual activity—.'

'What did they eat?' I interrupted.

A few faces smirked. Trust a woman to ask that, especially just as we were getting to the sex part. Fuck, we'll be discussing shoes next if we let her say anything else.

'I presume the local police followed up on it?' I continued. 'Like if it was snapper, then which restaurant served snapper on the night?'

The boss shrugged. It was his favourite way of side-stepping concerns. 'Detective work is not your area. You are supposed to profile the perp, not the dining scene.'

All the brown noses chuckled obediently.

The meeting went on and on. The first victim was in Invercargill, way down at the southern tip of the South Island. The second one in Dunedin, moving up north along the east coast. And now the third in Christchurch, as though the killer were taking a sightseeing trip of New Zealand's cities, starting right at the bottom and continuing up the tourist map.

The conference room chair felt like an anthill. I just wanted to be left alone with the evidence. Three victims, all prostitutes. No trace of sexual activity. I knew that was telling. I just wasn't sure yet *what* it was telling me.

That evening, when I'd climbed the stairs to my flat, I found a letter stuck into the tiny space between the door and the jamb. I recognised the handwriting in the single word on the envelope. I read the letter three times, cried twice, then went inside, smoothed out the sheet and put it deep in the knickers drawer, together with all the others.

That night, I dreamt about my ex. I don't call him by his name anymore. All that's important is his status: he was mine once, and now he isn't.

The 4th one, Wellington

I was right. The bastard is travelling up the map. Yesterday he crossed over to the North Island and did the capital city.

I had a busy week. First, I got to fly around the country, checking the dinner lead in Invercargill, Dunedin and Christchurch. Invercargill was sunny and cold, Dunedin was Scottish and cold, and Christchurch was its usual twee self.

I got several gourmet meals out of it, all compliments of the taxpayers, but no restaurant could recall seeing any of the murdered girls. Most owners shook their heads 'no' before they even glanced at the photos. I can understand that—some publicity can be bad publicity. When news came of the Wellington murder, I didn't even bother with the restaurants, although I did fly in to examine the murder scene itself, which looked like the rest of the capital city: windy and wet.

Second, I worked out what we knew of the perpetrator so far. Most serial killings are about control and power and—yes—sexual pleasure, whether or not any sexual assault has actually taken place. The fact that he first stunned his victims could point to inferior physical strength, or to cunning in not wanting to leave evidence that would have resulted from a struggle, the most obvious being his skin under the victim's fingernails. Then there was the geographical spread of the killings: years of experience were shouting that this was an important clue.

Third, I analysed the victims. We use victimology to discover the motives of the killer—profiling the victims to profile the killer, so to speak. Four women, prostitutes, all wined and dined and sexually untouched. Why?

I compared the photographs of the four. No obvious physical similarities, although all the victims were of European descent and on the plump side. I noticed that last point because my mental image of a call girl is slim curves and legs as slim as a man's, not the familiar portly lines I see in the mirror every night. There were no further points of intersection. The hair, for example, ranged from sandy to mousy, and there was nothing in the faces to suggest a fetish for small noses or heavy jaw lines or freckles.

'Cupcake, meet your new assistant,' the boss's head was in my cubicle again, peering over the partition. How was I supposed to concentrate with him asking for progress updates every five minutes? 'His name is Neil.'

'What bloody assistant?'

'This isn't arson or a series of petty thefts, Cupcake. It's murder.'

'Gee, thanks. I wouldn't have noticed myself.'

The boss shrugged—I know because I saw

one of his shoulders bob over the partition. 'I'll leave you two to get acquainted.'

My new assistant (he must be short not to show above the partition, I mused, as I kept my eyes on the latest pathology report) entered the cubicle and settled his arse comfortably between my coffee mug and the photographs. I raised my head from the paperwork in a studied theatrical gesture.

A sudden jolt. Heart in mouth. Knees that buckled even though I was sitting. Breathe, girl, breathe. Take a good look. See, the resemblance is just superficial.

'Hi,' he said. Fortunately, the voice was nothing like my ex's.

'Bugger off, Nick. This is my case.'

'Neil.'

'Yeah, whatever.'

*　　*　　*

I'd met my ex at a party. It was more of a booze-up than a party, really, which is not exactly my scene. I sat on the porch with a bottle of mineral water and wondered what to do with the rest of my Saturday night.

'Has anyone ever told you how gorgeous you look when you frown?' said a voice behind me.

For a pickup line, it wasn't the worst. And as the evening progressed, I discovered that he had a knack for words and always said the very thing I wanted to hear. I went home with him that night.

He was a dream to listen to, but crap in bed.

'I know there are two things I excel at,' he said when he was done. 'This, and my job.'

I chose not to comment on the excelling-at-this part. 'What's your job?'

'Chess instructor. You?'

'I'm with the police,' I didn't go into the details of freelance contracting. 'A criminal profiler.'

We spent the rest of the night talking about my work and what an amazing person I was. By the time the sun came up, I was in love.

*　　　*　　　*

'So what do you make of the locations?' Neil was still perched on my desk.

'A tourist perhaps. Or a businessman. Or a trucker.'

'I don't mean the geography. I mean the back streets.'

I hadn't considered that. 'He drove her there ostensibly to have sex? Nah, doesn't gel, they were too high class to do it in the street, be it business or pleasure. Plus, they weren't even killed in a car. They were killed in the street.'

'Exactly,' Neil's mouth said. His mouth looked so much like . . . I couldn't concentrate.

*　　　*　　　*

When my ex drove me to his flat that first night, he asked: 'What are you thinking right now?'

'That I hope you're not planning to kill me. Or if you are, that you'll at least have the decency to fuck me first,' I answered. I had no idea where that came from. I mean, true, he was a stranger and I was riding in his car through deserted streets, but still. The job's shadow on my private life, I thought.

'I've never killed anyone,' he replied gravely.

Something inside me churned. What sort of a comment was that?

'Well, that's good,' I replied.

'I started a few fires, though,' he added.

I flinched. Many serial killers play around with arson before they move onto murder. Arson allows the offender to feel the power and control, to observe the flames and the smoke and the commotion he created.

'By accident, of course,' he said.

*   *   *

'I guess we both need to chew on it,' Neil jumped off my desk. 'I'll be next door if you need anything.'

What I need, I reflected, is to know why the killer is not sticking to one city, thank you very much. And why he's targeting prostitutes.

*   *   *

'Have you ever been paid for sex?' he asked. We were lying in bed, but it wasn't afterglow. Despite ten minutes of vigorous pounding, I'd failed to get off, and, strangely enough, so had he. I faked. He didn't.

'No,' I laughed. 'Have you?'

'Me? You reckon I should be paid?' But it wasn't a question.

I ducked the issue. 'I meant, have you ever paid for sex?'

'That would be disgusting.'

So why mention it, I thought.

He pulled me towards his chest. 'You're the most beautiful person I know,' he whispered into my hair. 'We are soul mates. I want to be with you forever.'

I forgot the lousy sex and the weird conversation. I thought my heart would break with so much happiness.

I split up with him a month later.

*   *   *

The 5th one, Palmerston North

'We simply have to stop him before he gets to Auckland.'

'Why? There are no major cities north of us,' it slipped out of my mouth before I could stop it, so I followed up with 'sir.'

'Ah, Miss Profiler.' No *Cupcake* today. 'Will we be able to make positive id based on all your sight-seeing of the last fortnight?'

'Yes.'

'Oh?'

'I just need one more day.'

In fact, I only needed one email.

Before the meeting, as soon as I'd heard the news of the fifth murder, I looked up New Zealand chess championships on the Internet. As I suspected, they had been taking place in Palmerston North in the last couple of days. I couldn't find anything for Invercargill or Christchurch, but there had been an informal chess tournament in Dunedin on the exact day when the murder took place.

'Very well. One more day.'

*   *   *

I split up with him when he tried to kill a pigeon.

We were sitting on a park bench, an idyllic picture of thigh to thigh and hand in hand. A few birds pecked at the ground nearby.

'Shoo, shooo,' he shouted. Then his hand left mine and picked up a large stone.

I was quicker. 'Don't!'

He held me close. 'You have such a kind heart. You are a truly wonderful person. I don't deserve you. I'm evil.'

It was my turn to say all the right things.

I did.

But that night I split up with him.

A week later, the first body was found.

136

Neil squeezed my arm in the corridor.

'Sure you know what you're doing? We haven't had a chance to catch up and I've discovered a few clues—'

'I'm sure. But thanks.'

'Any time. You know where—'

'To find you, yes. Now, I have an email to write.'

I had to type in his email address from memory because I'd deleted it from the address book when we broke up. The message itself was simple. I outlined the current case, I presented the facts and the profile, I accused him.

Then I sat in front of my screen waiting for the reply.

'Sorry to bother you—'

'Bugger off, Neil.'

'At least you remember my name now,' a quick wink, so quick I may have imagined it. 'Listen, there is something you absolutely have to take a look at. I've been wondering about the locations, and then it hit me. There is an airport in every one of the cities where the killings took place—'

'The cities? What about the back streets? That was your big idea.'

Neil waved his hand. 'Didn't pan out. We probably won't know until we have him. If then. Perhaps he has a cul-de-sac fetish, who knows? Meanwhile, it was your idea of geographical locations that struck gold. I first thought ports and sailors, you know, because the stereotype kind of goes had in hand with prostitution—'

'But Palmerston North is not on the sea, so then you did a mental jump to airports?'

'Exactly. I checked all the aircrews stationed in the cities during the key times. One name is on every list.'

I was off my feet. 'Did you check out his background? How well does he fit the profile?'

'I left that for you. You're the expert.'

By the end of the day, we had our man. Just like I'd promised the boss.

He was a pilot, a small guy with big issues.

But not nearly as big as the issues I had. Talk of egocentric: I imagined that just because I ditched a guy, he'd go on a killing spree. Yeah right.

I'd almost screwed up my first big case.

But all the facts fitted: cruelty to animals, the fires, the ego, the problems in bed. The typical profile of a potential serial killer, if I ever saw one.

I was still sitting in front of the computer, typing in the final report and telling myself what an idiot I'd been, when the email came.

'I understand where you're coming from,' my ex said. 'And your email has given me an idea. An idea I'm very excited about. Let's have dinner tonight so that we can develop it further.'

Such simple words. I didn't know why they sent a shiver down my back.

'You're still here?' Neil smiled as he squeezed into my cubicle. It was a kind smile. I didn't know how I could ever think there was any resemblance to . . . to *him*. 'Fancy grabbing a bite to eat?'

'No thanks,' I heard myself say. My tongue was dry. 'I already have dinner plans.'

A Blow on the Head

Peter Lovesey

Almost there. Donna Culpepper looked ahead to her destination and her destiny, the top of Beachy Head, the great chalk headland that is the summit of the South Downs coast. She'd walked from where the taxi driver had left her. The stiff climb wasn't easy on this gusty August afternoon, but her mind was made up. She was thirty-nine, with no intention of being forty. She'd made a disastrous marriage to a man who had deserted her after six weeks, robbed her of her money, her confidence, her dreams. Trying to put it all behind her, as friends kept urging, had not worked. Two years on, she was unwilling to try any longer.

Other ways of ending it, like an overdose or cutting her wrists, were not right for Donna. Beachy Head was the place. As a child she'd stayed in Eastbourne with her Gran and they came here often, 'for a blow on the Head', as Gran put it, crunching the tiny shells of the path, her grey hair tugged by the wind, while jackdaws and herring-gulls swooped and soared, screaming in the clear air. From the top, five hundred feet up when you first saw the sea, you had a sudden sensation of height that made your spine tingle. There was just the rim of eroding turf and the hideous drop.

On a good day you could see the Isle of Wight, Gran had said. Donna couldn't see anything and stepped closer to the edge and Gran grabbed her and said it was dangerous. People came here to kill themselves.

This interested Donna. Gran gave reluctant answers to her questions.

'They jump off.'

'Why?'

'I don't know, dear.'

'Yes, you do. Tell me, Gran.'

'Some people are unhappy.'

'What makes them unhappy?'

'Lots of things.'

'What things?'

'Never mind, dear.'

'But I do mind. Tell me what made those people unhappy.'

'Grown-up things.'

'Like making babies?'

'No, no, no. Whoever put such ideas in your head?'

'What, then?'

'Sometimes they get unhappy because they lose the person they love.'

'What's love?'

'Oh, dear. You've such a lot to learn. When you grow up you fall in love with someone and if you're lucky you marry them.'

'Is that why they jump off the cliff?'

Gran laughed. 'No, you daft ha'porth, it's

141

the opposite, or I think it is. Let's change the subject.'

The trouble with grown-ups is that they always change the subject before they get to the point. For some years after this Donna thought falling in love was a physical act involving gravity. She could see that falling off Beachy Head was dangerous and would only be attempted by desperate people. She expected it was possible to get in love by falling from more sensible heights. She tried jumping off her bed a few times, but nothing happened. The kitchen table, which she tried only once, was no use either.

She started getting sensuous dreams, though. She would leap off the cliff edge and float in the air like the skydivers she'd seen on television. If that was falling in love she could understand why there was so much talk about it.

Disillusion set in when she started school. Love turned out to be something else involving those gross, ungainly creatures, boys. After a few skirmishes with over-curious boys she decided love was not worth pursuing any longer. It didn't come up to her dreams. This was a pity because other girls of her age expected less and got a more gradual initiation into the mysteries of sex.

At seventeen the hormones would not be suppressed and Donna drank five vodkas and went to bed with a man of twenty-three. He said he was in love with her, but if that was love it was unsatisfactory. And in the several relationships she had in her twenties she never experienced anything to match those dreams of falling and flying. Most of her girlfriends found partners and moved in with them. Donna held off.

In her mid-to-late thirties she began to feel deprived. One day she saw the Meeting Place page in a national paper. Somewhere out there was her ideal partner. She decided to take active steps to find him. She had money. Her Gran had died and left her everything, ninety thousand pounds. In the ad she described herself as independent, sensitive and cultured.

And that was how she met Lionel Culpepper.

He was charming, good-looking and better at sex than anyone she'd met. She told him about her Gran and her walks on Beachy Head and her dreams of flying. He said he had a pilot's licence and offered to take her up in a small plane. She asked if he owned a plane and he said he would hire one. Thinking of her legacy she asked how much they cost and he thought he could buy a good one secondhand for ninety thousand pounds. They got married and opened a joint account. He went off one morning to look at a plane offered for sale in a magazine. That was the last she saw of her husband. When she checked the bank account it was empty. She had been married thirty-eight days.

For a long time she worried about Lionel, thinking he'd had an accident. She reported him missing. Then a letter arrived from a solicitor. Cruelly formal in its wording, it stated that her husband, Lionel Culpepper, wanted a divorce. She was devastated. She hated him then and knew him for what he was. He would not get his divorce that easily.

That was two years ago. Here she was, taking the route of so many who have sought to end their troubles by suicide. Some odd sense of completion, she supposed, was making her take those last steps to the highest point. Any part of the cliff edge would do.

She saw a phone box ahead. Oddly situated, you would think, on a cliff top. The Samaritans had arranged for the phone to be here just in case any tormented soul decided to call them and talk. Donna walked past. A short way beyond was a well-placed wooden bench and she was grateful for that. She needed a moment to compose herself.

She sat. It was just the usual seat you found in parks and along river banks all over the country. Not comfortable for long with its slatted seat and upright back, but welcome at the end of the stiff climb. And it did face the sea.

In a moment she would launch herself. She wasn't too scared. A small part of her still wanted the thrill of falling. For a few precious seconds she would be like those sky-divers appearing to fly. This was the way to go.

Revived and resolute, Donna stood and checked to make sure no one was about. Perfect. She had the whole headland to herself.

Well, then.

What it was that drew her attention back to the bench she couldn't say. At the edge of her vision she became aware of a small brass plaque screwed to the top rail. She read the inscription.

In memory of my beloved wife Donna Maria Culpepper, 1967–2004, who loved to walk here and enjoy this view.

A surreal moment. Donna swayed and had to reach out and clutch the bench. She sat again, rubbed her eyes, took a deep breath and looked a second time because she half wondered if her heightened state of mind had made her hallucinate.

The words were just as she'd first read them. Her name in full. She'd never met anyone with the same name. It would be extraordinary if some other Donna Maria Culpepper had walked here and loved this view. The year of birth was right as well.

Two things were definitely not Donna. She hadn't died in 2004 and the way her rat of a husband had treated her made the word 'beloved' a sick joke.

Was it possible, she asked herself now, still staring at the weird plaque, that Lionel had paid for the bench and put it here? Could he have heard from some mistaken source that she had died? Had he done this in a fit of conscience?

No chance. Freed of that foolish infatuation she'd experienced when she met the man and married him, she knew him for what he was. Conscience didn't trouble Lionel. He'd had the gall to ask for a divorce—through a solicitor and after weeks of silence. He was cowardly and callous.

How could this bench be anything to do with Lionel, or with her?

It was a mystery.

Cold logic suggested there had been another Donna Maria Culpepper born in the same year who had died in 2004 and had this touching memorial placed here by her widowed husband, who was obviously more devoted and considerate than Lionel. And yet it required a series of coincidences for this to have happened: the same first names, surname, date of birth.

She took another look. In the bottom right corner of the plaque was a detail she hadn't noticed—the letters 'L.C.'—Lionel's initials. This, surely, clinched it. The odds against were huge.

She no longer felt suicidal. Anger had taken

146

over. She was outraged by Lionel's conduct. He shouldn't have done this. She had come here in a wholly negative frame of mind. Now a new challenge galvanized her. She would get to the truth. She was recharged, determined to find an explanation.

First she had to find him. After their break-up she'd had minimal contact, and that was through solicitors' letters. She had no idea where he lived now.

She walked down the path towards the town.

The Parks and Recreations Department at Eastbourne Council said that about forty seats had been donated as memorials by members of the public. A helpful young woman showed her the records. The bench had been presented last spring. A man had come in with the plaque already inscribed. He'd particularly asked for a teak seat to be positioned at the top of Beachy Head. He'd paid in cash and left no name, though it was obvious he had to be a Mr Culpepper.

Donna asked if he'd left his address or phone number and was told he had not. She took a sharp, impatient breath and explained about the shock she'd had. The clerical assistant was sympathetic and said it could only be an unfortunate duplication of names.

While Donna was explaining why she thought it couldn't be coincidence, an assistant at the next desk asked if they were talking about the seat at the top of Beachy Head. She said a few months ago she'd had someone else in, a woman, asking about the same seat and the man who presented it.

'A woman? Did she say why?' Donna asked.

'No, but she left her business card. I put it in the folder, just in case we found out any more.'

The card had slipped to the bottom of the folder. Donna was given a pencil and paper to make a note of the name and phone number. *Maggie Boswell-Jones, Starpart Film, TV and Theatrical Agency, Cecil Court, Off Charing Cross Road, London.* There were phone, fax and e-mail numbers.

Donna didn't have her mobile with her. She hadn't intended using it on this last day of her life. She used a public phone downstairs.

The conversation was all very bizarre.

'You're Lionel's wife? But you're dead,' Maggie Boswell-Jones said. 'You were killed in a flying accident.'

'I promise you I wasn't,' Donna said. 'I'm who I say I am.'

'How can you be? There's a seat on Beachy Head with your name on it. Lionel put it there in your memory.'

'He ran out on me in the second month of our marriage. May I ask why you were looking for him?'

'Because he's my boyfriend, darling, and he's missing.'

Donna felt as if she'd been kicked in the stomach. She knew Lionel was a rat. Now she knew he was a two-timing rat. He'd walked out on her and started up with this woman. She made an effort to save her fury for Lionel.

'How did you know about the seat?'

'He took me up there specially. He wanted me to know that you were dead. I made it very clear to him that I don't get involved with married guys. He spoke nicely of you.'

'Look, can I come and see you?'

'Is that necessary?'

'I'm determined to find him. With your help I'm sure I can do it.'

*   *   *

At the agency Donna recognised a man who stepped out of the lift. He was an actor she often saw in *Coronation Street*. In the waiting room upstairs there were framed movie posters. In a glass showcase were various awards, including what looked like an Oscar.

Maggie appeared high-powered with her black fringe, tinted glasses and purple suit, but she turned out to be charming. Coffee and biscuits were ready on a low table in her office. They sat together on a black leather sofa. 'I've been trying to understand what's going on with Lionel ever since you phoned and I'm still at a loss,' Maggie said. 'He's such a bright guy. I can't think how he got to believe you'd passed away.'

'He made it up,' Donna said.

'Oh, I don't think so. He said the kindest things about you. I mean, why would he go to the trouble and expense of buying a seat for you?'

'To fool you into believing I was dead and he was free to have an affair. Can't you see that?'

Maggie took a lot of convincing. Clearly she was still under Lionel's spell. Just as Donna had believed him incapable of leaving her, so Maggie insisted he must have lost his memory in the flying accident.

'There was no flying accident,' Donna said. 'He talked about taking me in a plane, but it never happened. He took ninety thousand pounds from our account.'

'Really? This shocks me.' The colour had drained from Maggie's face. 'I certainly need to find him because I lent him sixty grand to renovate a house he'd bought for us in the south of France.'

'You'll never see that money again,' Donna said. 'He's a conman. He befriends women like you and me and fleeces them. If you don't mind me asking, how did you meet him? Was it through a newspaper?'

'What a skunk!' Maggie said, and Donna knew she'd got through to her at last.

That evening Maggie took Donna for a meal at a restaurant near the agency. 'I'm not short of a bob or two,' she said, 'but let's admit it, I'm unattached and on the lookout. I meet plenty of hunky blokes in my job, but it doesn't do to mix work and pleasure, so I put my ad in *The Guardian*. Lionel was the best of the bunch who responded—or seemed to be.'

'I wonder how many other women he's conned,' Donna said. 'It really upsets me that he went to all that trouble to make out I was dead and he was a free man. There must be some way of stopping him.'

'We can't stop him if we can't find him.'

'Couldn't we trace him through the newspaper?'

'I don't think so. They're very strict about box numbers. And they cover themselves by saying you indemnify the newspaper against all claims.' Maggie thought for a while, and took a long sip of wine. 'Righty,' she said finally. 'What we do is this.'

*   *   *

GORGEOUS Georgie, 38, own house, car, country cottage, WLTM Mr Charming 35-45 for days out and evenings in and possible LTR. Loves fast cars, first nights and five star restaurants.

'What's LTR?'

'Long term relationship. That should do it,' Maggie said.

'It's a lot more pushy than mine,' Donna said.

'How did you describe yourself?'

151

She blushed a little. 'Independent, sensitive and cultured.'

'Independent is good. He's thinking of your bank balance. But we can't use it a second time. This will pull in quite a few gold-diggers, I expect. We just have to listen carefully to the voice messages and make sure it's Lionel.'

'I'll know his voice.'

'So will I, sweetie.'

'And who, exactly, is Gorgeous Georgie?'

'One of the best stuntmen in Britain.'

'A *man*?'

'Ex-boxer and European weightlifting champion. He's been on my agency books for years. He'll deliver Lionel to us, and the money he stole from us. When Georgie has finished with the bastard he'll beg for mercy.'

*   *   *

Maggie called ten days later. 'He's fallen for it. A really unctuous voice message. Made me want to throw up. He says he's unattached—'

'That's a lie.'

'Professional, caring and with a good sense of humour. He'll need that.'

'So what's the plan?' Donna asked.

'It's already under way. I got my film rights director to call him back. She has the Roedean accent and very sexy it sounds. I told her to play the caution card. Said she needed to be certain Lionel isn't married. He jumped right

152

in and said he's a widower and would welcome the opportunity to prove it. They're meeting for a walk on the Downs at Beachy Head followed by a meal at the pub.'

'Your rights director?'

'No, silly. She was just the voice on the phone. He'll meet Georgie and get the shock of his life. All you and I have to do is be there to take care of the remains.'

Donna caught her breath. 'I can't be a party to murder.'

'My sense of humour, darling. Georgie won't do anything permanent. He'll rough him up a bit and put the fear of God in him. Then we step up and get our money back.'

* * *

Maggie drove them to Eastbourne on the day of the rendezvous. She took the zigzag from Holywell and parked in a lay-by with a good view of the grass rise. From here you wouldn't know there was a sheer drop. But if you ventured up the slope you'd see the Seven Sisters, the chalk cliffs reaching right away to Cuckmere Haven. It was late on a fine, gusty afternoon. Georgie and the hapless Lionel were expected to reach here about five-thirty.

'Coffee or champagne?'

'You *are* well prepared,' Donna said. 'Coffee, I think. I want a clear head when we meet up with him.'

Maggie poured some from a flask. 'We'll save the champers for later.'

Donna smiled. 'I just hope it stops him in his tracks. I don't want other women getting caught like we did. I felt so angry with myself for being taken in. I got very depressed. When I came up here I was on the point of suicide.'

'That's no attitude. Don't ever let them grind you down.'

'I'm not very experienced with men.'

'Well, at least you persuaded the bastard to marry you, darling. You can't be a total amateur. Me, I was conned every which way. Slept with him, handed him my money, accepted his proposal.'

'Proposal? He proposed to you? Actually promised to marry you?'

'The whole shebang. Down on one knee. We were engaged. He bought the ring, I'll say that for him. A large diamond and two sapphires. He knew he had to chip in something to get what he wanted. What did it cost him?—a couple of grand at most, compared to the sixty he got off me.'

'I had no idea it got that far.'

'He'd have married me if I hadn't caught him out. Bigamy wouldn't have troubled our Lionel.'

Donna was increasingly concerned about what she was hearing. 'But you *didn't* catch him out. When I first phoned, you called him your boyfriend. I had to persuade you that he was a conman.'

'Don't kid yourself, ducky,' Maggie said with a harder edge to her voice. 'I knew all about Lionel before you showed up. I had him checked out. It's easy enough to get hold of a marriage certificate, and when he gave me the guff about the flying accident I checked for a death certificate as well, and there wasn't one, so I knew he was lying. He was stupid enough to tell me about the memorial bench before I even saw it. I went to the council and made sure it was bloody Lionel who paid to have it put there. He handed them the plaque and a wad of cash. What a con. He could go on using that seat as his calling card every time he started up with a new woman.'

'If you knew all that, why didn't you act before? Why are you doing this with me?' Donna said.

'Do you really want to know?' Maggie said. She reached for the champagne bottle and turned it in her hands as if to demonstrate good faith. 'It's because you would have found out. Some day his body is going to be washed up. The sea always gives up its dead. Then the police are going to come asking questions and you'll lead them straight to me.'

'I don't know what you're talking about.'

'Get with it, Donna dear. Lionel is history.'

She felt the hairs rise on her neck. 'You killed him?'

'The evening he brought me up here to look
155

at the stupid bench. I waited till we got here and then told him what an arsehole he was. Do you know, he still tried to con me? He walked to the cliff edge and said he would throw himself off if I didn't believe him. I couldn't stand his hypocrisy, so I gave him a push. Simple as that.'

Donna covered her mouth.

'The tide was in,' Maggie said in a matter-of-fact way, 'so I suppose the body was carried out to sea.'

'This is dreadful,' Donna said. She herself had felt hatred for Lionel and wanted revenge, but she had never dreamed of killing him. 'What I can't understand is why we're here now—why you went through this charade of advertising for him, trying to find him—when you knew he was dead.'

'If you were listening, sweetie, I just told you. You knew too much even before I gave you the full story. You're certain to shop me when the police come along.'

It was getting dark in the car, but Donna noticed a movement of Maggie's right hand. She had gripped the champagne bottle by the neck.

Donna felt for the door handle and shoved it open. She half fell, trying to get out. Maggie got out the other side and dashed round. Donna tried to run, but Maggie grabbed her coat. The last thing Donna saw was the bottle being swung at her head.

The impact was massive.

She fell against the car and slid to the ground. She'd lost all sensation. She couldn't even raise her arms to protect herself.

She acted dead, eyes closed, body limp. It wasn't difficult.

One of her eyes was jerked open by Maggie's finger. She had the presence to stare ahead.

Then she felt Maggie's hands under her back, lifting. She was hauled back into the car seat. The door slammed shut. She was too dazed to do anything.

Maggie was back at the wheel, closing the other door. The engine started up. The car bumped in ways it shouldn't have done. It was being driven across the turf, and she guessed what was happening. Maggie was driving her right up to the cliff edge to push her over.

The car stopped.

I can't let this happen, she told herself. I wanted to die once, but not any more.

She heard Maggie get out again. She opened her eyes. The key was in the ignition, but she hadn't the strength to move across and take the controls. She had to shut her eyes again and surrender to Maggie dragging her off the seat.

First her back thumped on the chalk at the cliff edge, then her head.

Flashes streaked across her retina. She took a deep breath of cold air, trying to hold on to consciousness.

She felt Maggie's hands take a grip under her armpits to force her over the edge.

With an effort born of desperation she turned and grabbed one of Maggie's ankles with both hands and held on. If she was going, then her killer would go with her.

Maggie shouted, 'Bitch!' and kicked her repeatedly with the free leg. Donna knew she had to hold on.

Each kick was like a dagger-thrust in her kidneys.

I can't take this, she told herself.

The agony became unbearable. She let go.

The sudden removal of the clamp on Maggie's leg must have affected her balance. Donna felt the full force of Maggie's weight across her body followed by a scream, a long, despairing and diminishing scream.

*   *   *

Donna dragged herself away from the crumbling edge and then flopped on the turf again. Almost another half-hour passed before she was able to stagger to the phone box and ask for help.

When she told her story to the police, she kept it simple. She wasn't capable of telling it all. She'd been brought here on the pretext of meeting someone and then been attacked with a bottle and almost forced over the edge. Her attacker had tripped and gone over.

Even the next day, when she made a full statement for their records, she omitted some of the details. She decided not to tell them she'd been at the point of suicide when she discovered that bench. She let them believe she'd come on a sentimental journey to remember her childhood. It didn't affect their investigation.

Maggie's body was recovered the same day. Lionel, elusive to the end, was washed up at Hastings by a storm the following October.

He left only debts. Donna had expected nothing and was not discouraged. Since her escape she valued her life and looked forward.

And the bench? You won't find it at Beachy Head.

Tell Me

Zoë Sharp

'So, where is she?'

Crime Scene Investigator Grace McColl ducked under the taped cordon at the edge of the crime scene and showed her ID to the uniformed constable stationed there.

The policeman jerked his head in the direction of the band shelter as she signed the log. 'You'll have your work cut out with this one, though,' he said.

Grace frowned and moved on. She was already dressed from head to foot in her disposable white suit and she made sure she followed the designated pathway, picking her way carefully to avoid undue contamination.

The girl was on the stone steps in front of the band shelter, no more than sixteen years old but still a child, with dirty blonde hair. As Grace approached she could see the girl had her thin arms folded, as though hugging herself against the cold. And she must have been cold, to be out in the park in this weather in just a mini skirt and a skimpy top. Unless, of course, he'd taken her coat with him when he'd left her . . .

Over to the right, the rhododendron bushes grew thick and concealing. It might have been

160

Grace's imagination, but she thought the girl's eyes turned constantly in their direction, as though something might still lurk amongst the glossy foliage.

She squatted down on her haunches next to the girl and waited until she seemed to have her full attention.

'Hello,' she said quietly. 'I'm Grace. I'm going to be taking care of you now. Can you tell me who you are?'

There was a long pause, then: 'Does it matter?'

Grace eyed her for a moment. The girl might have been pretty if she'd taken a little time, a little care. Or if someone had taken a little care over her. Her hair was badly cut and her fingernails were bitten short and painted purple, the varnish long since chipped and peeling.

'Of course it matters,' Grace said, keeping her tone light. 'Finding out about you will help us find out who did this to you. Help us to catch him. You want that, don't you?'

' 'Spose.' The girl shrugged, darting a little glance from under her ragged fringe to see if her attitude achieved the desired level of sullen cool. The action revealed the livid bruise, like spilt ink on tissue, that had formed around her left eye.

Grace tilted her head, considering. 'He caught you a belter, didn't he?' she murmured.

'I bruise easy,' the girl said, suddenly

161

defensive now. 'And I'm clumsy.'

'Don't tell me,' Grace said, setting her bag down and opening it. 'You were always walking into doors at home, falling down the stairs.' She shook her head. 'Did no-one stop to wonder?'

The girl's face darkened. 'They knew, all right,' she said. 'They just didn't give a—'

'No,' Grace said dryly. 'I can see that.' She pulled out evidence bags and swabs, and paused. 'Is that why you ran away—ended up on the streets?'

The girl's head jerked up and she looked at Grace fully for the first time, scowling. 'Who said I'm living rough?'

Grace regarded her calmly. 'Your clothes are dirty enough,' she said.

'What do you expect?' the girl snapped. She gestured angrily towards the rhododendrons. 'Being dragged through the mud, having him—' She broke off, bit her lip, looked away.

'Your clothes were dirty before that,' Grace said, no censure in her quiet voice. 'And you're a pretty girl. Your nails are painted—or they were. You wouldn't have done that if you hadn't wanted to look nice, once upon a time.'

The girl's lip curled. 'That's for fairy stories.'

'Mm,' Grace said. 'Let me see your hands.'

Reluctantly, the girl put both hands up, backs towards Grace, fingers splayed rigidly. Grace almost smiled at the defiance she read there, taking hold of one carefully in her

162

gloved fingers, scraping out minute debris from under the receded nails.

'Ah-ha,' she said, under her breath. 'You got a shot in, I see. Marked him. Oh, well done, you.'

The girl looked unaccountably pleased at this praise and it occurred to Grace that she must have received very little by way of approval in her short life. She thought of her own mother, who lavished praise and nurtured self-confidence in her only child. Ironic, then, that the pre-adolescent Grace had always been so desperate to win the approbation of her more distant father.

'*Your* father wasn't around much, was he?' she said absently, noting the time and date and case number on the evidence bag as she sealed it.

The girl scowled at her again. 'You're guessing,' she accused. 'No way can you tell that from looking at my hands.' Her mouth twisted into a sneer. 'Read tea-leaves as well, do you?'

'No,' Grace said levelly, 'but I've been doing this job long enough to recognise the other signs.'

The girl took her hand back and folded her arms, a challenge in her voice. 'So, go on,' she goaded. 'If you're so clever, *you* tell *me*. Who am I?'

'All right.' Grace sat back on her heels, oblivious to the activity going on around her.

163

She focused inwards, closing her eyes for a moment.

'You can't do it, can you?' the girl jeered.

Grace's eyes opened. 'Your father left when you were young,' she began. 'Your mother blamed you and lost herself in the bottle—pills or booze, or possibly both.'

The girl rolled her eyes, gave a derisive laugh. 'Oh, big deal,' she said. 'You could be talking about half the kids round here.' She jerked her head towards the nearby high-rise. 'Not good enough.'

'OK,' Grace conceded. 'Then you're going to tell me it's also obvious that your mother brought home a procession of one-night stands to pay the rent. How old were you when the first of them asked if *you* were for sale, too?'

The girl wouldn't meet her eyes. 'None of your business,' she muttered.

'Mm, I thought so.' She paused again but the girl wouldn't respond. 'But you didn't leave then, did you? You clung in there. For a while. Until it got too much and you attempted self-harm.'

'Who says I did?'

Grace nodded towards the old scars on the girl's wrists. 'You cut yourself,' she said, picking her words with care. 'Not a serious attempt, I don't think. A cry for help. But nobody answered, did they?'

The girl twisted the cheap ring round on her finger and didn't speak, staring across the

164

grass to where the row of uniforms swept the parkland.

'He listened,' she said at last, so quietly Grace hardly caught the words.

'Ah,' she said softly. 'Of course he did.'

The girl's head jerked up at the tone in her voice, eyes flashing. 'Don't say it like that,' she snapped, harsh. 'You don't know how it was. He loved me!'

'I'm sure he told you he did,' Grace said, bland. 'Gave you that ring, didn't he? Told you that you were his girl now. Just like all the others.'

'I was. I *am.*'

'So how long was it before he told you about the man he owed money to? About how it would all be all right if only you'd just have sex with this man. Did you refuse? Is that why he hit you?'

'I made him angry. He was sorry—after.'

'But he still made you do it, didn't he?'

'I wanted to help him. He didn't force me or nothing.'

'Not that first time, no,' Grace said. 'But that was just the beginning, wasn't it? When did you realise he wasn't your boyfriend any more, but your pimp? Or did you ever realise it?'

'If I'd had someone looking out for me,' the girl said, her voice bitter now, 'do you think something like this would've happened?'

'It might have done. If it was him—your boyfriend—who did this to you.'

165

The girl shrugged. 'Might have been,' she said, dismissive. Her glance was defiant. 'Might not.'

'So, was he a client?'

'Client?' the girl spat. 'Would that make it better for you if he was? Would that make it not so shocking, not so bad, if I was on the game? Oh well, just another hooker picked the wrong john. Had it coming.'

'No,' Grace said evenly. 'It would just give us a better place to start looking.'

'Yeah, right,' the girl snorted, still surly. 'You're thinking it, though. I can tell.'

'I try to keep an open mind but you're not making it easy for me. You shouldn't have been here at that time of night, you see. It's where the working girls come with the men they pick up when the clubs turn out. And you could have just been trying to make the money for your next fix.'

The girl opened her mouth, saw Grace's gaze on the evidence of her addiction that tattooed the crook of both arms, and shut her mouth again with a glower.

'You see too much,' was all she said.

'It's my job,' Grace agreed. 'Just as it's my job to find out who you are, and who did this to you. To stand for you, when no-one else would.'

The girl looked at her with doubt and speculation in her eyes for the first time. 'And you'll do that, will you?'

166

'I will.'

'Just for me?'

'Yes.'

The girl sighed. 'You'll be the first, if you do.'

'Well, better late than never, then.'

The girl was silent again. The sky had darkened overhead and she looked up into the gathering clouds. 'It's going to rain,' she said.

'I know,' Grace said. She stood. 'I'd better get back to work. The rain will destroy the evidence if we don't protect the scene quickly.'

The girl nodded. 'You'll be back, though, won't you?' she said. 'You won't leave me?'

'Of course,' Grace said. 'They'll take you in, but you'll certainly see me again. I'll need more from you, if we're to catch him.'

'That's good,' the girl said and gave a small smile, rusty from lack of use.

'How are you getting on, Grace?' asked a brisk voice from behind her. Grace turned to see one of the Detective Constables who'd just arrived on scene. She bent and snapped her bag closed, then straightened.

'I'm about done,' she said.

'Will you get anything useful from her, do you think?'

Grace glanced back.

The girl lay on the damp steps, arms wrapped across her body, in the position they'd first found her. Her eyes were open and glassy, her lips tinged with blue. The marks of the stranglehold that had killed her showed dark and ugly around her throat.

'I think so,' Grace murmured. 'The dead always talk to me in the end.'

Jizz

Mat Coward

'Definitely, hundred per cent. I'd know him anywhere.' I didn't mention that I probably wouldn't recognise an elephant halfway across the lounge bar without a long squint and a broad hint, and I didn't remind them that I hadn't seen the man they called Target One since I was fourteen. That was their problem.

Anyway, to be fair, there was something about the bloke: his walk, perhaps, or the set of his nose. Something about him was familiar. They say that every cell in the human body is replaced every seven years, so that none of us is ever the person we used to be, but even so I was confident in my identification of Target One.

Half an hour later I was back behind the flap at the club, serving lunchtime pints to the old boys. 'Please form an elderly queue,' I told them, as they jostled for their turn. I can't stand customers waving furled banknotes at me, waggling their eyebrows, calling out: 'When you're ready, Warren.' I'm a barman, not a pole dancer.

I'd signed DCI Hoad in as a guest, and he sat there now, in a nook by the fruit machine, not watching me work. Reading a paper, eating a Scotch egg and ignoring a half of lager.

The phone at the far end of the bar rang; someone asking for Rabbit. I called out 'Rabbit,' a couple of times, then told the woman on the phone that Rabbit wasn't in.

'Thanks, lad,' said Rabbit. I know the drinkers only by their pub names. It's a matter of professional courtesy.

'He's supposed to be in the supermarket,' one of Rabbit's drinking companions told me. 'She ought to try ringing there.' The whole table chortled, the bags under their rheumy eyes shaking more than their shoulders did.

Just before the end of my shift, DCI Hoad brought his glass up to the bar. It had finally emptied, possibly by evaporation. We do keep the club warm, out of respect for our core clientele. 'Just wanted to say thanks for your help today, Warren,' Hoad said, his voice low and casual. 'Much appreciated.'

'Want to tell me what he's done?' I asked.

Hoad sniffed. He was a tall man with hairy cheekbones. 'Naughty acts. In historical times.'

'You're not local, are you?' I said, wiping the counter with a cloth.

'Was that not explained to you?'

Since it had been Hoad who had done what little explaining had taken place, the question was redundant. I answered it anyway. 'No, not really.'

'We're part of what's called a Long-Term

Pursuit Team. We take over looking for fugitives, when the detectives previously seeking them give up on them—because too much time has passed, or because all leads have gone cold.'

'What, you just carry on looking for them forever?' It was a romantic idea, I thought; bit sinister, too.

'Mostly, we get involved when new information is received.'

'New information?'

'His ex-wife finds out he's got a slag,' Hoad explained, 'so she dobs him in.'

'Oh. Not, like, analysing ear-prints and that?'

Hoad shook his head. 'No. Slags, mostly.'

I smiled, wiped on. Something I've often wondered about plainclothes police: they show you those cards to prove who they are, but if you've never seen one before how are you supposed to know if it's genuine?

*   *   *

When I was a kid, we took in lodgers. I loved it. Our house wasn't big—mid-terrace, no garage and almost no garden—so it got a bit crowded during wet weekends, and if you wanted to have a crap on a workday morning you had to book a week in advance, but I was sure it was more fun than my schoolmates' lives.

New people all the time, a decent proportion of them weird. A majority of them foreign, because as far as they knew *all* British rooms were that small, and because they believed my mother when she acted offended about the cornflakes: 'No, no, *no*, Signor! Cooked breakfasts are *Irish*, not English. That's like calling a Belgian a Jew and then offering him your pork scratchings, but I accept your apology because how could you know any better? Tuck in, the milk's fresh.'

You've got to have interest in life. An interest, some interests, but above all *interest*. That's what I learned from my childhood among the lodgers: to pity people whose lives lack interest. Comings and goings, noises and hushes, changing faces and involuntary placings: without all that, I'd walk around all day fast asleep. I am the one person in a thousand who, if a guy says 'We're the police, young man: could you help us with our investigations?', I'll say 'Let me get someone to cover the bar for me, we can start right now.'

The day after I'd identified Target One, they took me out again to have another look. I sat in the back with DCI Hoad. There was a young woman in the passenger seat, and the driver was a middle-aged bald man.

'Do birds watch telly through their feet, do you suppose?' I asked Hoad.

'What?'

172

'I just wondered, perhaps that's why they spend so much time perched on TV aerials.'

The driver cleared his throat. 'Nothing on at this time of day, though, is there?' he said. 'Unless they're all wife birds, watching rubbish all day long instead of doing the precious little that they're supposed to be doing.'

We all went hummingly quiet after that. Except the driver, who continued clearing his throat like a pit pony on its final day.

'There we go,' said DCI Hoad, nodding my attention towards a betting shop, and the greatcoated man who was coming out of it. 'We've got to be certain. Take another look. You still sure that's him?'

I studied the striding figure as best I could at that distance, and in the brief time available. 'That's him,' I said. 'Unmistakeable.'

The DCI didn't say anything. He left it to the woman sitting next to the driver. She said: 'Warren, that's a different bloke.'

*   *   *

Very few young people drink in the club, and even then 'young' means under the age of fifty-five. Hornpipe is one of the youngest: thick grey hair down past his big shoulders, military bearing, torso slim as a girder, naval pipe. He left early that evening: one rum, two pints, a single fill of ready-rubbed.

'You off then, Hornpipe?' I asked him, when

173

I saw that he was off. 'Got a tip too hot to wait?'

He winked. 'I'm on a fat-finding mission.'

'He's got a new girlfriend,' one of the rheumy-eyed old boys told him, though presumably he already knew. 'Feeding him up, isn't she?'

Hornpipe smiled a proud admission. 'Curry with all the trimmings tonight. Mustn't be late. Give us a bottle of white, will you, Warren? Not too dry.'

'Chips?' the old boy asked.

Hornpipe nodded. '*All* the trimmings,' he said.

As Hornpipe swung his shoulders through the exit, the old boy leaned over to me. 'Ladies' fingers,' he said. 'That was always my favourite.' I smiled and polished my specs; a laugh, if unsolicited, can cause confusion in the hospitality trade. If you're really unlucky, it can cause hospital.

My favourite lodger was an Italian student called Fred. He was with us for nine weeks when I was ten. When her friends asked my mother what the Italian boy was studying, she'd say, 'Oh, nothing, love—only economics.' He was a quiet and seemingly characterless fellow, and I don't suppose he addressed more than twenty words to me all the time he was there. He was my favourite because he couldn't tell the difference between 'Hello' and 'Goodbye.' He knew there *was* a

174

difference—and let's face it, he had a fifty-fifty chance of getting it right at random—but throughout those nine weeks, every single time he entered a room he said 'Goodbye,' and every single time he left he said 'Hello.' It is hard to imagine anything which might make a ten-year-old boy happier.

During a lull, DCI Hoad put a quiet question to me. 'What you got against the thin guy with the grey hair, then?'

'Evening, Chief Inspector,' I said. 'Didn't see you come in. Can I get you a drink?'

'Jonathan So-and-So,' said the DCI, without recourse to any written note, 'date of birth such-and-such, address blah-blah, no previous convictions, divorced, railwayman retired early on health grounds.'

'He gets more women than I do,' I said, 'if that's what you mean. But most of them aren't ugly or married, so we're not really in competition.'

'Was he ever a lodger at your mum's?'

'Not to the best of my—'

'So why did you pick him out, earlier on, coming out of that betting shop?'

That was interesting. I polished my specs.

'Don't polish your specs, Warren,' said Hoad. 'You don't need to make a point, I know you're shortsighted, I see your specs every time I look at your nose. But you're not actually blind, are you? In a registered sense?'

There was no genuine annoyance in his

175

voice, which also interested me. 'I'm not making a point,' I assured him. 'I'm just polishing my specs.' I polished some more, just to make a point. 'This job you do—must be hard coming up with evidence, years after an event?'

Hoad zipped his jacket. 'Depends what you're looking for,' he said.

*   *   *

He was only there two nights, but the lodger called Applegate taught me all I ever learned from other people about birdwatching. Anything else I learned over the subsequent years—if there was anything else—I taught myself. He introduced me to the idea of knowing a bird by an overall sense of its identity, rather than by recognising text-book characteristics. This was the bit that made the hobby interesting to me, the only bit really, and all that kept me interested in it well into my late teens.

Whenever a new lodger moved in, I'd go and bother them. That was what my mother called it: 'Don't go bothering the lodgers, Warren.' Some of them enjoyed being bothered more than others. Applegate, the special birder, was amongst the most welcoming of all.

'What is special birding?' I asked him, when he'd told me that was why he had the compact binoculars and the miniature camera. I expected his reply to involve a humorous reference to sexual matters, and made ready a polite smile. Instead, he astounded me.

'It's not the birds,' he said. 'It's where you see them.'

The place or type of place, he meant. If you'd never seen a starling at a county cricket ground, then as soon as you spotted one at the Oval you'd tick it off. But if you'd seen starlings at every county ground bar Taunton, then you'd need a starling at Somerset to complete your list.

Or Buckingham Palace, for instance. 'I've never had a pigeon in the grounds of Buck House,' he told me, sitting by the gas fire in his room at my mum's. He was young, with collar-length hair and hollowed-out cheeks.

'Buck House?'

'Funny thing. I've had sparrows there, I've had a long-tailed tit—I've had a parakeet, believe it or not. Never a pigeon. Don't ask me why. There must be pigeons there. Unless he shoots them—even then, he couldn't shoot them all, surely?'

He wouldn't convince me that he'd been special birding in the grounds of Buckingham Palace, not that first night. I asked him to, but he wouldn't. He saved that for the second night.

Next time I saw DCI Hoad in the club—three days after my initial identification—he told me what they wanted Target One for. I could have insisted he tell me the first time we met, but I found it interesting to see how long he could go without telling me.

'Armed robbery,' he said, apropos of nothing at all, unless you count a diatribe against fancy crisps and a nostalgic interlude concerning the little blue salt packets of his childhood. 'Not round here, up in Scotland, way up near Dundee. Money van. Your man,' he said, tilting his glass at me, 'your mum's onetime lodger, fled. His accomplices were taken at the scene, three of them. But your man was never captured.'

'This was how long ago?'

'Ten years, ish.'

'Long time ago,' I said. 'He'd be out by now. Was the stolen money recovered?'

DCI Hoad took a dry sip from his half of lager-top. 'This was *armed* robbery we're talking of, let me stress: a thuggish undertaking from beginning to end. As ungentlemanly a crime, I've always thought, as mugging. As ungentlemanly as flashing, I've always felt. They think they're aristocrats, armed robbers do, and in a way they're right, in that they have nothing but contempt for those who work for a living.'

'A very bad business,' I agreed.

'Now your man is back in London,' said Hoad, 'and we mean to take him.'

'That man,' said an old boy by the bar, when Hoad had left, 'is suffering—I don't want to worry you—he's suffering from obsessive-compulsive disorder.'

'He is?'

'Haven't you noticed? He always wears matching socks.'

'Right. Good spot.' I wondered if it was a clue, but it wasn't, it was just the old boy being a boastful scruff bag. And, of course, old boys look downwards more than they look upwards, which is why their shoes are always cleaner than their lapels.

'Don't mean to offend you, if he's a mate of yours,' the old boy added, 'but you need to take care.'

'Agreed.'

'Because they can smile if they try, but a leopard cannot change his socks.'

*   *   *

When Applegate did tell me his secret of special birding, I was momentarily unsure whether it was disappointing or thrilling. I decided to be thrilled, because that was likely to yield more interest.

'It's a simple law,' he told me, when I went bothering him on his second night in our house, the night before he left. 'How I get into the particular places—sports venues, government offices, whatever you like—to do special birding. It's this: if you walk far enough, search long enough, and look hard

179

enough, sooner or later you will always find a hole in the fence.'

'Always?' I asked.

'A gate carelessly unlocked, a guard post briefly unmanned, there's always something.'

'*Always?*'

'I've never been defeated,' Applegate told me, simply. 'Yes, always—but sometimes you'll have to keep looking for it for years on end. It isn't easy, it's just simple.'

'It might not be so interesting if it was easy,' I said and Applegate agreed.

'People are always surprised when a bomb goes off or a leader gets shot, and there's always an enquiry followed by a resignation, but what people don't understand is that security cannot exist in the physical world: it exists only on the symbolic level.'

'Have you ever had a chaffinch at the Archbishop of Canterbury's gaff?'

Applegate smiled, and gave me two chewy mints. 'It's on the list,' he said, which could have meant yes or no.

*　　　*　　　*

There is absolutely nothing wrong with my hearing, but at first I thought DCI Hoad had said 'He tickles their foxes.' Then I realised that he was speaking jargon, and I was able to translate: 'He ticks all the boxes.'

'He does?'

'The man you identified as your mother's former lodger. If you were to lay him on top of Target One, there would be no discernible overlap. The profile is a natural match.'

'So he's your fugitive, then? But you say I identified the wrong man the second time?'

'Ah, well,' said Hoad, nudging a beer mat along the counter with his half of brown ale. 'Do me a favour, and forget anyone ever mentioned him. All right?'

'Must have been a nuisance for you, though, me making that inexplicable error.'

'Especially,' said Hoad, 'don't mention it to your thin friend himself, OK? Don't want him suing us for wrongful identification. You laugh, but I've seen it happen.'

The Greeks have a word for that, I thought. But mostly they're too polite to use it.

*   *   *

From the betting shop, I followed Applegate to a snooker club. He wasn't playing, just sitting at the bar drinking a cup of coffee. His hands trembled, and his day-beard looked as if it had been tattooed into the hollows of his face. He didn't look as if he'd spent the last decade golfing on the Costas.

'How did you know me?' he asked.

'By something that was indefinably you,' I said, and it was the honest truth. When DCI Hoad first approached me, he'd showed me a photo of Target One and asked if I knew him. I'd said yes, that the man had lodged with us briefly about ten years ago. Would I recognise him if I saw him now, did I reckon, all this time later? I said I was sure I would, I recalled him well. That was good, according to Hoad, because they'd checked, and I was the only traceable being on earth who might be able to perform that particular public service.

The photo was taken, it looked to me, very close to when he'd lodged with us, going by his age and hair. Perched in the snooker club now, the funny side of the bar for once, I wondered where they'd got it from: it looked formal, posed, not a barbecue snap—the eyes were scared, not drunk. In any case, I had no hesitation in identifying both the picture of Target One, and the man sitting next to me, as Applegate, our former lodger.

'Yeah,' said Applegate, nodding his head, clearly delighted that I had remembered something he'd taught me when I was a kid, delighted perhaps to be recognised at all by someone, and for something, from his previous life. 'Yeah—I remember you.'

I was a bit taken aback. It had never occurred to me that he might not remember me. I'd only ever met him before when I was a boy, and things like that don't occur to boys, only to men, which is why being a man is not all it's cracked up to be.

'I saw you coming in here,' I told him, 'and I

thought it was you. Thought I'd just say hello, see if you remembered me.' I smiled. 'Do you still go special birding?'

Applegate drank some more coffee, and took a while over it even though his cup was empty. 'No, no. Not really, haven't really had much chance lately.'

Ever since Applegate's two nights at my mum's, I have never relied on my poor eyesight to recognise people, or birds, or anything further away than my fingers. I use the indefinable. I knew that on both occasions when I had identified Target One for the police, I had shown them Applegate. So it was, at the very least, interesting to wonder why they wanted me to think that I had picked out Hornpipe the second time.

*   *   *

At closing time that evening I asked Hornpipe, since it was a Tuesday, if he was on for our semi-regular game of billiards once I'd locked up. Afterwards, we'd generally get a Chinese or an Indian and eat it in my flat above the club.

'Sorry, mate,' he said, 'I'm seeing Maggie tonight.'

'No problem. How's it going with her?'

He filled his pipe. 'Slowly, carefully. You know me, Warren—I always hit the ground walking. Took her to the pictures on Sunday.'

'What did you see?'

'Dunno.' He shrugged. 'Something with explosions in it.'

'Any good?'

'It didn't bust my blocks, but she seemed to like it.'

I got him another rum, and said: 'That guy you've seen me talking to lately, he's a cop. Quite interesting really. He's with a unit that goes after jobs from years back. You know, tracking down the takings from old robberies, pursuing villains who got away, all that.'

He lit his pipe. 'What do they want with you? Something you've not been telling us, Warren?'

I shook my head. 'Case of mistaken identity. No, I've never been inside, myself. Did three weeks, once, in a youth offender's, but that's not prison, is it?' In the couple of years between Mum dying and me landing my first proper girlfriend I did manage to generate a fair bit of paperwork, but nothing a reasonable person could class as authentically post-adolescent.

'How about you?' I asked, taking care to ensure that my tone invited a jokey reply. 'You ever been arrested?'

A jokey response was what I got, indeed. 'Wasn't my fault. The sign by the till said "I'm being trained, please bare with me".' The joke didn't really work until he'd spelled it, which a better comic might have known is always a bad sign.

'I suppose it's only right,' I said, pouring myself a light ale. 'No matter how long after the event, they should still go after robbers, murderers, whatever.'

He let his pipe go out, and watched it as it did so. 'In Iraq,' he said, 'when the Americans take over a town—strategically, or for purposes of collective punishment—the first place they seize isn't the armoury or the town hall or the barracks. It's the city hospital. They arrest staff, beat them, humiliate them—to prove to the world that they're terrorists, you see? Because if they weren't terrorists, obviously they wouldn't do that to them, so that proves they're terrorists. Medicines are destroyed, equipment is vandalised. A picket of soldiers is set up outside the hospital to prevent doctors getting out to treat the wounded, or supplies getting in. Snipers on rooftops fire at anyone approaching the hospital for treatment. Any ambulance seen moving round the town, they shoot out the driver, leave the van to burn.'

Which was interesting, and I was wondering, long-term, what becomes of all those snipers when they're out of the army and back in Boise? I opened my mouth to say as much, but Hornpipe ran me over.

'Once that has happened, Warren, then nothing, ever again, anywhere in the world, is a crime. Crime no longer exists. A rape, a

185

murder, an arson—if you say those still exist, then you are forgiving the snipers.'

Rape, murder, arson: he didn't mention armed robbery, I noticed. I started to speak again, but apparently it still wasn't my turn. Hornpipe put his pipe in his leather-lined pocket. 'Belsen, Hiroshima, Fallujah. Nothing else has ever happened in this world—those are the only three events ever. Anyone who pretends to investigate any other event is making a terrible joke and is not deserving of your respect, Warren.'

When he'd gone, a previously unnoticed old boy said to me, 'I wonder how much of that old loot gets handed in, when the cops find it? I mean, it'd be a matter of percentage, wouldn't it—if you hand in more than fifty per cent, you're not really corrupt.'

'Were you eavesdropping?' I said.

'No, son—I was listening. You could never accuse me of eavesdropping. The state of my vertebrae puts a bar on any form of lurking.'

*   *   *

On my way to the snooker club on Wednesday afternoon, I wondered if my mother was ever questioned about Applegate. If she had been, she'd never mentioned it to me, and I hadn't been, but it seemed sense that if you were sniffing after a fugitive you'd check his previous addresses and talk to those who'd

186

spent time in his company.

Applegate said he wasn't really living anywhere. He answered in a way that suggested he'd once been ashamed of this fact, but that now he couldn't remember what the point of being ashamed had been.

'Where do you sleep? You must at least sleep somewhere.'

'I ride the night buses. They're very good these days, much better than they used to be.'

'You can doss on my floor, if you like, while you're getting sorted.'

For a moment he looked puzzled, but then he seemed to remember that he'd once met me for a few hours ten years earlier, and so that explained everything. Just to make sure, he said: 'Serious?'

'Long as you don't tell anyone; it's not strictly legal. I'm not allowed lodgers.'

'Few things are,' said Applegate, retrieving an overnight bag from behind the bar. 'Strictly legal. And fewer every year.'

After the club closed, and I'd let Applegate in via the delivery door, we ate a curry on my sofa. 'I'm sorry to hear you gave up the special birding,' I told him. 'I loved all that. Not even a pelican in the governor's garden?'

He went bright red and fanned his mouth as if the Chicken Mild was on fire. 'A pelican!' He laughed.

Not making anything of it, I asked him when he'd got out.

'Couple of weeks.'

I assumed he must have thumped someone inside quite badly to serve such a long sentence. Couple of someones, possibly. No wonder he never got a crack at the governor's garden. 'What brought you back here? Family?'

He gave up on the curry. Belatedly, I realised that it really was too hot for him, after what he'd been eating since his youth ended, and I fetched him a glass of milk. 'No family here, or anywhere else, though I mostly grew up round here. No nobody, anywhere, truth is.'

I didn't think that was the truth—it lacked the indefinable qualities of truth—but it was probably too close to be worth a quibble. 'So, why here?'

He poured the milk down his throat, and smiled. 'I was hoping your mum had kept my room for me.'

'The old house has gone, mate—street's gone. They demolished it for a car park, for a new shopping experience. But the shopping experience didn't happen, so nor did the car park.'

'You surprise me,' said Applegate. 'Seems to me people love the parking experience so much, you'd think they could open a car park in the middle of a desert and it'd fill straight up.'

'It's a brownfield site now,' I explained. 'They'll put housing on it as soon as they get the legals untangled. So, if you left anything at my mum's I'm afraid it's gone.'

'Damn!' He said, still smiling. 'I suppose I'll just have to give in and buy a brand new toothbrush.'

'In the house, that is. The back yard's still there, such as it was.' I finished my curry, and put the kettle on.

Applegate said: 'She was a very pleasant woman, your mother, but I have to say her breakfasts were disappointing.'

*   *   *

I hadn't seen DCI Hoad for a little while now. Not that I was expecting to see him, but it was interesting even so. I had the feeling he was keeping in touch, though, in his own way. One night when Hornpipe's new girlfriend had an evening class in something amusing, I invited him upstairs after closing for a game of cards. 'Friend of mine'll join us,' I said. 'We can have a proper game.'

When the two men saw each other, their shocked and mutual recognition was obvious to any onlooker. Applegate, delightedly and rather innocently, said: 'Hello, mate!'

Hornpipe worked all expression off his face, before turning to me. 'Well, young man—is this you being interesting again?'

I held up a hand for silence and said: 'Changed my mind. Let's go down the

189

snooker, instead. So we can talk freely of interesting things.'

Two minutes after opening time in the morning, Hoad was at the bar. He had a pea-sized blob of shaving foam on one earlobe, and I wondered if he'd left it there or put it there. He looked tempted to raise his voice to me, so I went in first.

'Is it legal to put recording devices in innocent people's private residences?'

He wiped the shaving foam off. Possibly it had started to itch in the warmth of the club. 'Is that a quiz question, Warren, or you planning a change of career?'

'You wanted to use me, Chief Inspector, as a kind of medium who contacts the living. You wanted me to bring those two together in my flat merrily chatting about the missing money from the robbery, while you skulkily earwigged. So unless you were hidden in the wardrobe, you've bugged my flat.'

He told me if I could find the bug I could keep it; which, as so often, could mean yes or no. I told him: 'One man did get away after the robbery, but it wasn't our old lodger, Applegate. He was arrested at the scene and has been in prison ever since.'

'Ah yes, I can explain that,' said Hoad, 'we lied to you.'

'Oh well, fair enough, then.' I polished my specs to a fine point.

'I'm a detective, not a vicar. You're a nice

190

lad, Warren, but if I think it serves the interests of justice, I will lie to you, I will lie to more than a dozen frail nuns, and I will show my hairy bottom to your grandmother through a patio door on her ninety-second birthday.'

'I'll hold you to that,' I said. 'Cheaper than a bouquet, and it's the sort of gift that lasts all year.' I put my glasses back on, and poured DCI Hoad a small bottle of brown, on the house. 'You think Hornpipe is the missing man. Recent intelligence, possibly. But you can't prove it. No-one's ever given him up, whoever he is, and Applegate is your last chance. You have to get a statement from Applegate or a confession from the fugitive. After all this time there won't be any other evidence.'

'So did you have your chat last night?' Hoad asked. 'The three of you, old friends?'

I ignored that, and I'm sure Hoad expected me to. Just because you bug a man's flat doesn't mean you think he's an idiot. 'You know that Applegate has no-one left on the outside. If he ever had anyone. You'll have checked his prison visiting records, letters in and out and all that. You could only hope that he'd come back to this area, and that he'd make contact with Hornpipe. To collect his long-deferred wages.'

'The other two robbers died in prison,' Hoad said. 'One heart attack (crack), one suicide (divorce). Your two chums are all that's left.'

'You got the spottiest person in your office to crosscheck the two of them, and this borough. One common factor: I live here, work here, grew up here, and can claim acquaintance with both men. Without even pausing to thank the computer bloke, you convene a meeting: we've got this Warren guy, how do we use him?'

'I've got a sort of cousin who's a vicar,' Hoad admitted, 'but I've never actually met him.'

I didn't need to polish my specs, or the club's glasses, or to wipe an ashtray or rub the sell-by dates off a box of crisps, because I'd ticked all this off on my fingers late last night. The crime was a long time ago; the police lied to me; Applegate has served his full sentence and so doesn't deserve any additional grief; Hornpipe is a decent bloke with a girlfriend, whatever his past, and in any case all his cells are new ones now; the cops are only after the money and they bugged my flat. And first, they misunderstood me: if I ever desire money that badly, shoot me.

'I asked the boys last night,' I told Hoad. 'They say there isn't any money.'

'They don't want to share it,' Hoad said. 'We do. We want to share it with you.'

'They say the man who got away, got away with nothing.'

He nodded. 'Which is what you expected them to say.'

I nodded. I could hardly deny something so obvious, and retain any credibility as a barman.

'Or,' said Hoad, 'alternatively, you could just accept the solemn word of a sworn officer, when he promises you on his mother's life that he is as bent as a sharp turn.'

It was several hours later, while serving a generic old boy with an imperial stout, that I realised there really wasn't any money, after all. Not according to logic there wasn't, anyway.

If any of the robbers knew where the money was, it would have to be the man who had successfully fled the scene with it: the man who got away. Now, even supposing the untaken man is the most honest criminal in the world—after ten long winters, would he really still be waiting for his workmates to get out before he retrieved the bulging holdall? Especially when two of them are dead, and the third's a sorry dosser.

When Applegate told me he'd only come back to this area because it was where he'd spent most of his childhood, he was telling the truth. The police had wanted me to think they were after the money, chasing a private pension fund, but that wasn't what they were after. So what was?

*   *   *

I had to wait for the DCI's attention, even

after he'd escorted me through the security door, while he checked something to do with another case. He asked a uniformed PC how the interview was going.

'It's tricky, guv,' the constable replied. 'She doesn't speak very good English.'

Hoad looked puzzled. 'I thought she was English?'

'She is, guv, she just doesn't speak it very well.'

Once we were alone, I told him: 'You're not corrupt.' He looked offended, or annoyed. It's probably not the sort of bitter accusation that detectives are used to facing. 'You led me to believe there was money to be had, so that I'd have a motive for getting those two chatting— and if I thought you were bent, I'd ignore any oddities in your story. Like you told me Applegate was the fugitive, not Hornpipe, because I didn't know Hornpipe back in his era, so you could hardly rope me in by asking me to identify him from an old photo.'

'We're not bent,' Hoad said. 'Are you very disappointed?'

'You know, Chief Inspector, it wasn't a great plan. If they ever announce a TV show called the Fifty Greatest Foolproof Plans of All Time, don't get in a load of champagne and canapes and ask your high-flying brother-in-law and his stuck-up wife round to watch it. You'll only embarrass yourself. What were you planning to do if it didn't work?'

Hoad made a dismissive noise through his teeth. 'Plans don't exist. The only people who have plans—with all the bits worked out—are mentals. Guy who carries out a massacre because the CIA is sending messages to his tonsils—*he's* got a plan, perfect plan, every detail checked and double checked, but sane people just ask themselves: if we do *this*, is there a decent chance of *that*? And if everyone in the car nods, you go ahead and do it.' He scratched one of his hairy cheekbones. 'Or grunts. I prefer nods, but then canteen chat has it that I'm a bit of a snob.'

'Why are you after Hornpipe?'

'Two of them are dead, Warren. One of them's served his time. And the last one spends his afternoons stinking your club out with his rum and his pipe, and his evenings escorting a large-bottomed woman to see badly-made films in an air-conditioned environment.'

'It was ten years—'

'Ten years ago, during the robbery, a shotgun was discharged. Probably by human error, to be fair, but discharged all the same. An employee of the robbed company, a working man like you and me, lost a leg and one eye.'

I sat down. Uninvited, which is generally the best way in a cop shop. 'He's still alive?'

'He tried to top himself when his daughter emigrated to New Zealand, but it's not that

195

easy with one leg and one eye. You try getting a rope round your neck, when you can only see in 2-D and you keep hopping off the edge of the chair.'

'That's a bad business,' I said, thinking that if you don't work in the hospitality trade, telling is often more effective than hinting. And also thinking that some crimes do still exist, no matter how many times you change your cells per decade. 'Chief Inspector—I told Applegate and Hornpipe everything I knew.'

Hoad couldn't resist, apparently: 'Or *thought* you knew. Yes, I know—Applegate's decamped.'

'Why's *he* run? He's served his sentence.' It wasn't as unfair as falling off your own scaffold, but it seemed rough justice all the same.

'Same reason he's been living rough since he got out of nick, I suppose. He's entitled to housing help if he wants it, evidently he doesn't want it. Make your own diagnosis.'

I did. 'He could have walked out of prison any time he wanted.'

'I doubt it, the places he was held.'

'I reckon he could,' I said. 'But to spend time looking for a hole in the fence, you've got to really want to find it. Hornpipe hasn't fled?'

'Nope, latest reports have him sitting at your bar patiently waiting for you to serve him. Long nerves as well as broad shoulders. No wonder he gets the women, eh?'

'You'll never get them talking now. They'll be on their guard forever. I'm very sorry, Mr Hoad.'

'You mean you're very embarrassed, Warren. But are you sorry Hornpipe isn't going to prison?'

I gave it due consideration. 'Not sure. If you could put the man who ordered Hiroshima in prison right now, dig him up and jail him, would you?'

DCI Hoad pointed to the sign taped to his office door: Long-Term Pursuit Team 7. 'The clue's in the title, son,' he said.

*   *   *

I poured Hornpipe his drink, as polite as ever, and when I asked him 'Who pulled the trigger?' he answered in similarly civil vein.

'No-one *pulled* the trigger. Someone fell over, stumbled.'

'And the gun just went off?'

'No, Warren.' He sighed and put his pipe down. 'See sense—that wouldn't be nearly comical enough. It seems the stumbler grabbed at the man next to him, instinctively, as he fell. That man, in the interests of safety in the workplace, tried to pull his gun-cradling arm *away* from the falling man's clutch.'

I pictured it, and got it. 'Which, in the great tradition of irony that has bedevilled your generation since Altamont, had the effect of tightening his finger and discharging the firearm.'

'So I'm told,' said Hornpipe, before raising his voice slightly and adding: 'Of course, I wasn't there myself. But one might imagine that's why none of the gang was ever willing to name the fugitive. Because the whole thing was accidental—as well as youthful and moronic—and they wouldn't wish to add anyone's woe to their own.'

'I take your point, but I'm not sure how it applies to the one-legged, one-eyed, unemployable man.'

'*Wish* to add, I said,' Hornpipe stressed. 'There's got to be a difference between deliberate and accidental acts, or else why did we bother with all that evolution hoo-hah?'

He was arrested six days later, sitting right there at the bar, halfway through filling a pipe which, I imagine, he will never smoke again. In fact, I know he won't: I saw one of the uniformed boys slip it into his tunic pocket, presumably as a souvenir.

*   *   *

'You got some tapes after all? Are they legal evidence?'

'We didn't get any tapes,' Hoad told me, 'and we were never interested in court evidence. Only in cop evidence.'

I didn't ask him what the difference was, so

198

that he was forced to tell me.

'Stop polishing those bloody things, Warren. There were those of us in the review team who believed that Hornpipe was the man, and there were those who didn't.'

'Your driver didn't,' I guessed.

Hoad laughed. 'He owes me a fiver.'

'The only evidence you were looking for was something to take to your bosses?'

'In any bureaucracy, Warren, the real job is convincing line management to let you do what you think you need to do. The rest is just overtime.'

'And now you've convinced them?'

'You have, Warren. Applegate running was enough to justify us scraping Hornpipe's scabby surface. That brought us enough to authorise a more subcutaneous look. That brought us enough to get an arrest. Now we continue digging towards a charge. I don't know how much tax you pay, Warren, but I hope it's plenty because we've just spent a shitload and we're going to need some more.'

I asked one of the old boys in the club, 'Is your identity indefinably the same at seventy as it was at seven, no matter how many cell-changes you've got through in the meanwhile?' I didn't really think it was: I thought Hornpipe wasn't the same person, but that by contrast the one-eyed man was. There was only one portion of justice available, and one of them would have to go without—either the man who'd long since sloughed the robber's skin and didn't deserve a belated punishment, or the time-frozen innocent who still deserved the redress he'd needed ten years ago.

'Dunno,' said the old boy, 'but I always knew Hornpipe was dodgy.'

'Did you? How?'

He shook his head and twinkled his sticky eyes, a better comic than poor old Hornpipe. Unwilling to lean too heavily on a predictable punchline, he just said: 'What other sort do you get in this place?'

Out of her Mind

Carla Banks

Words on a page, black print on white. Words on a screen, black print on a flickering monitor, safe, contained. He's the dark shape in the night, the soft footsteps that follow in the darkness, sealed away as the book is closed, fragmenting into nothing as the screen shuts down into blackness.

But now he's seeping around the sides of the screen, bleeding off the edges of the paper . . .

The room is empty. The light reflects from the walls, glints on the metal of the lamp. The screensaver dances, flowers and butterflies, over and over.

*   *   *

The summer heat was oppressive. Laura looked out of her window. The small patch of ground behind the house was scorched and wilting, and over the fence, the buddleia that grew in the alleyway drooped, its purple flowers brown at the tips.

The air was still and dry. The louvers were open, but the wind chimes she had put there at the beginning of the summer hung motionless.

201

She tapped them with her finger, the gentle reverberation giving her the illusion of coolness.

'You going to sit there all day?'

Laura jumped and turned round quickly. It was David.

'You going to be sitting in front of that thing all day?' He resented the hours she spent in front of the screen.

'I was just . . . ' She gestured towards the monitor where the screen saver danced in a pattern of butterflies. 'It won't come right. I need to . . .' She couldn't explain, but she knew she needed to keep on writing.

He was impatient. 'It's beautiful out there. I'm not going to be stuck in on a day like this. I'm going out. Are you coming?'

She looked round the room. Her study was stark with its north facing window and bare walls. Her desk was tucked away in a corner. It was quiet. It used to be safe. 'I have to go on. I can't leave it now.' And she couldn't.

'You aren't doing anything. You're just staring out of the window. Can't you make an effort, pretend you want my company once in a while? I might as well be married to a machine.' He was angry and frustrated. It was summer, a glorious summer's day, and Laura just wanted to sit in her study, staring at the white flicker of the screen, tap tapping her fantasy world into its electronic soul.

You married a writer, she wanted to say. *That*

was the deal. But there was no point. He didn't want to hear it.

'I'm going.' He slammed out of the room, out of the house, doors opening and closing with noisy violence. Laura let the silence close in on her, then turned back to her desk. Her hand hovered over the mouse for a second, then she pushed it, and the screen saver cleared.

*   *   *

Writing running down the screen. Just words on a page. And then a shadow when the house is empty, a footstep in the corridor, the creak of someone outside the door.

It's nothing. It's imagination. He's always been there, the monster under the bed, the bogey man in the cellar. Just a shadow to frighten children in the night.

Only the footsteps are gone now. There is no monster under the bed, no bogey man in the cellar. He used to live in Laura's mind, live on her screen, in the pages she writes. He used to hide behind the butterflies and the flowers of the screensaver. But now he's gone. He's escaped. He's somewhere else.

The butterflies used to dance on the buddleia, but now the flowers are dying and the butterflies have gone.

Laura was in the supermarket. While David was out, she could surprise him. *Look, I did the shopping!* He hated shopping. Mechanically, she took stuff off the shelves, loaded it into the trolley, a bag of salad, bread, eggs, milk, bacon. Something was tugging at the back of her mind. She could see the patterns on the screensaver moving and dancing. Waiting. She shouldn't have left. She had to hurry, she had to get back.

The supermarket aisles were long and well-lit with rows of shiny tins and boxes reflecting the light into her eyes. Reds and yellows and greens, primary colours, nursery colours. The trolley had a red plastic handle and bars of aluminium and the boxes and bottles and tins on the shelves flickered as the bars ran past them, like the flicker of the words on the screen.

The aisles were long and straight. Laura pushed the trolley faster and faster past each one. Biscuits and cakes. Tinned fruit and vegetables. Soaps and cleaning stuff.

And a movement at the far end of the aisle.

She squinted but the light reflected off the tins and the bottles, reflected off the shiny floor. She screwed her eyes up, but she couldn't see it properly. It had been—just a flicker, a silhouette moving quickly round the corner, out of view, out of sight.

She pushed her trolley into the next aisle, and her foot slipped in something sticky, something viscous, something that spattered across the shelves and dripped onto the floor, red, dark, *drip, drip*, pooling round her feet in abstract patterns.

She stopped, frozen, half-hearing the voices: 'Look out, someone's dropped a bottle of wine . . . better be careful . . . mind the glass . . . get a . . . '

She pushed past, the wheels of her trolley smearing through the red and leaving a trail on the floor behind her. 'Hey!' But the voices didn't matter. She had to get back.

The queue snaked away from the checkout. She pushed her trolley to the front. 'Sorry, so sorry . . .' as people stepped back, frowning, puzzled, too polite to object. She didn't have time to queue. She fed her purchases through and dug in her bag for her purse as the checkout girl drummed her fingers on the till and the queue stirred restlessly behind her.

'. . . with a filleting knife.'

She blinked. It was the girl sitting at the till, her face hostile and blank. 'What?'

'Forty five. Forty five pounds . . . Did he slash her?'

'What?'

The eyes rolled in exasperation. 'D'you want any cash back?'

'Oh. No.'

The car park dazzled in the sun, the concrete hot under her feet, the metallic paint of the cars sending shards of light into her eyes.

*   *   *

Night time. He walks the streets, he waits in the dark places. A silk scarf whispers between his fingers. It's light and gauzy, patterned with flowers and butterflies. It's smooth and strong. He has something else in his hand. It's long and thin and sharp. It glints where the light catches it.

Someone is coming. The sound drifts around the roadway, loses itself in the darkness, in the wind that rustles the tops of the trees. It's what he's been waiting for, tap, tap the sound of heels on the pavement, like the sound of fingers on a keyboard, like the sound of knuckles against the door. Tap, tap, tap. And then there will be the other sound, the sound that only the two of them will hear, the sound behind her in the darkness . . . the soft fall of footsteps, almost silent, lifted and placed, carefully but quickly, moving through the night.

*   *   *

The heatwave broke two days later. In the morning, the sky was cloudless, the shadows sharp as a knife on the walls and on the

206

pavements. The buddleia, parched, drooped down, the petals falling into the dust. Laura sat at the table crumbling a piece of toast between her fingers. The sun reflected off the polished surfaces, off the steel, off the cutlery, the spoons, the knives.

David sat opposite her, immersed in the paper he held up in front of his face. Laura stared at the print, black on white, words that would blur and vanish behind the moving patterns of flowers and butterflies.

'Maniac.' David closed the paper and tossed it onto the table.

Laura looked at the crumpled sheets. WOMAN . . . KNIFE ATTACK. She grabbed it and smoothed the page out, her hands moving in frantic haste.

WOMAN KILLED IN KNIFE ATTACK. It had been the previous night, in the car park, in the supermarket car park. The woman must have walked across the concrete that was still warm from the sun, her heels tapping briskly, the streetlights shining on her hair. Walking tap, tap, tap towards the shadows where the trees started, the trees that whispered in the night.

She went to her room and switched on her machine. Her hands hovered over the keyboard and then began to move. Tap, tap, tap. The words appeared on the screen, filled it, scrolled down and down as her hands flew over the keys. She wrote and deleted, wrote and deleted, and each time, a woman walked

207

into the darkness where gauze and flowers and butterflies fluttered in the wind. And the light glinted on something in the shadows, just for a moment.

The day greyed over as the clouds rolled in. The air cooled, became chill. Laura typed, deleted, typed again.

'Still at it? You've been here all day.'

She jumped and turned round.

It was David trying hard to be patient. 'I've made tea.'

'Thanks.' She wasn't hungry, but . . . 'Thanks.'

He'd made egg and chips. The chips lay pale and limp on the plate. The yolk of the egg trembled under its translucent membrane. She cut the chips into small pieces, pushed them into the egg, watched the bright yellow spill and spread over her plate.

'Egg and chips not good enough for you any more?' He was angry again. He'd made the effort and she didn't appreciate it—didn't appreciate *him*.

She couldn't explain. She couldn't tell him. 'It's fine. Egg and chips is fine. I'm just not hungry, that's all.'

He grunted, but didn't say anything. He was trying. He was making the effort. He shook the sauce bottle over his plate. *Smack* as he hit the base with the flat of his hand. She watched red spatter over the mountain of chips.

'Ketchup?'

208

She shook her head. 'Did you get a paper? Is there any more about . . . ?' *About the murder.*

'No. Stupid cow, though. What did she expect, out on her own at that time?'

What had she expected? She saw the wine spilled on the supermarket floor, the drip, drip from the shelves, the bright red of the splashes. David lifted a chip to his mouth. Ketchup dropped onto the table, *splat.*

She had to get back.

*   *   *

The dark footprints cross the paving stones of the alleyway, prints that look black and shiny in the moonlight, growing fainter and fainter with each step until they fade to nothing.

It is starting to rain. The drops make black marks on the dry flags. The drops are big and heavy, splashing out as the rain falls harder and harder. The footsteps begin to blur, and a darker colour trickles across the ground with the rain that starts to run across the path, across the alleyway, running into a black pool that gleams in the shadows. And the puddles cloud as dark streaks mingle with the clear water, running thick and black then clearer and faster, into the gutters, the drains and away.

*   *   *

The next morning, the sky was Mediterranean

blue. The sun blazed down, scorching away the freshness of the storm. The air was hot and dry. Laura's fingers flew across the keys.

David was the doorway. 'It's been on the radio,' he said. His voice had the lift of excitement. ' "There's been another.'

'I know.' She typed, the words spilling out of her fingers. She couldn't stop now, she mustn't stop . . . *and the rainwater ran across the paving stones* . . .

'Not the supermarket.' David wanted her attention. He had information to pass on, exciting news, and he couldn't wait to tell her. 'In the alleyway, Laura. They found her in the alleyway. Right behind our house! Last night.'

I know. But she couldn't say it.

*   *   *

Three a.m. Something wakes her. She lies very still and listens. Silence. The wind whips the clouds across the moon. Light. Dark. Light. Dark. The curtains are pulled back and the trees in the garden make caves of shadow. They rock and sway. The branches of the cotoneaster scrape across the window. Tap. Tap. Tap. The alleyway is full of night.

*   *   *

David had been out all day, came back to find Laura at her desk, the dishes unwashed, the fridge empty.

He looked at the screen. 'Nothing. You've done nothing. Sitting there all day. I can't do it all.'

Sorry. I'm sorry. But she couldn't say it. Her eyes moved towards the window, where the buddleia flowers drooped over the high fence. A sudden breeze made them lift their heads. A piece of tape, yellow and black, danced through the air and wrapped itself round the stems, then hung still. All day. She'd heard them there all day, behind the garden, in the alley.

Later, David relented. 'I've made you a sandwich.'

She couldn't choke it down.

'There's no pleasing you!'

She flinched as his hand brushed against hers.

His eyes were cold. 'Out. I'm going out. If you want to know.'

She couldn't worry about that now, couldn't let it distract her. Nothing else mattered now. She had to get back to her desk, back to her screen.

In the distance, she heard the door slam.

*   *   *

Laura sat in her study. The rain had started falling hours ago, and David had not come back. She read the words that filled the screen.

211

She scrolled down, read. Her fingers tap tapped on the desk. She looked through her window. Now, it was dark outside, the back garden, and the fence, and the alleyway all in shadow, empty now and silent.

She went out into the corridor and opened the hall cupboard. The corridor was painted white, the walls satin, the doors gloss. The floor was polished. The light reflected into her eyes.

She opened the cupboard. She drummed her fingers, tap, tap against the door. She took off her slippers, and put on a pair of black shoes, strappy, with very high heels. She had to fiddle with the fastenings for a few minutes. She stood up, tall and straight. She put on her coat, a mac, light and summery. It would be no protection against the rain. She threw a scarf, a summer scarf, thin and gauzy, round her neck. Then she walked to the door. Her heels tap, tap, tapped on the lino.

*   *   *

The street is long and straight, with pools of light under the streetlamps, light that glints off the water as it runs down the gutters. And between the lights, only shadows. The rain drips off the trees. Dark and then light. Dark and then light.

I can't find you any more!
I can't find you any more!

212

She walks on. She knows he will come. He has to.

Her feet tap tap on the pavement, moving quickly from light to light. And then she hears it. The sound of soft footsteps behind her, moving fast, moving closer.

Something glints in the darkness. Something blows in the wind, gauze and butterflies and flowers.

*　　　*　　　*

David gets home late. As he comes through the gate, he sees a curtain twitch in the house next door. He hesitates, then walks up the path. His own front door is open. He can hear it banging as the wind blows. He catches it before it can swing shut again, stands for a moment, listening. He looks at the window where the curtain moved. 'Laura?' he calls, and again, more loudly. 'Laura?' Then he closes the door quietly behind him.

The house is silent.

He goes to Laura's study. The screen flickers, the flowers and butterflies locked in their perpetual dance. He banishes them with a touch, and looks at the screen, looks at what Laura was writing, looks at the words that scroll down the screen.

The street was long and straight, with pools of light under the streetlamps, light that glinted off the water as it ran down the gutters. And between

213

the lights, only shadows. The rain dripped off the trees. Dark and then light. Dark and then light.

I can't find you any more!

And then, over and over: *No, no, no, no . . .* down the screen. Down and down, *no, no way, no way, no way. No . . . w no . . . w now now now.*

He reaches out and presses a key. The writing jumps, fades, is gone.

The black screen faces him.

He smiles.

Street Value

Frank Tallis

I was sitting in the Bankside bar, looking out of the window at a sluggish Thames. The water was black, like oil, and a fine toxic mist had begun to blur the City lights. Two helicopters swooped down low and followed the river, swinging a search beam from bank to bank. I took a drag from my cigarette and tried to relax.

Someone tapped me on the shoulder.

She was about fourteen, or maybe fifteen, I guess. They get younger and younger.

'Need anything?' She said, making a sign with her fingers that I hadn't seen before.

I looked her up and down: PVC, spiked hair, and a temple socket.

Reaching into my jacket I pulled out my ID and pushed it up against her nose. Of course, I was counting on her being able to read for the gesture to have the desired effect.

Fortunately, she could.

'Oh, right.' She whispered.

I didn't say anything. I just watched the blood drain from her face and her lower lip tremble. I jerked my head toward the door. For a moment she looked puzzled. Then, hardly believing her luck, she slowly backed off and disappeared into the crowd.

I could have booked her, but couldn't be bothered. In a few years everything will be different. In a few years neither of us will be here anymore.

*   *   *

Sure, there were rumours. I'd heard the words: Xanth, Gold, Saff, or just plain Yellow—heard about its double-take street value. (Yeah, yeah). Since legalisation every AWOL pharmacist in the enterprise zone was trying to find the next big thing. No self-respecting Soho-type would be seen doing Metropolitan. Getting high with the Mayor's approval? It just doesn't go with the territory. So, when I heard about Xanth for the first time I assumed it was going to be another Haze or Poke. A clever piece of spin engineered to make someone, somewhere, an ultra-fast Eurodollar. But then some of the boys said they'd seen things in the clubs: *Exchange, Clink*, and *Bermondsey Wall*. They pulled a few punters in for tests but the mini-lab results were inconclusive. Even so, my curiosity was aroused.

I spent a few nights hanging out at BW, and spotted three serious players—Kuczmierczyk, Arnie Rabinowitz, and Still Life. More importantly, I saw a few rich kids doing the 'breathing thing'. *Yeah*, I thought. *That's new*.

It was time to employ the services of Mr. Al-

Razzaq, so I requested authorization from the Chief. He got back to me the same day.

'Third time this year, Proctor.'

'Yes, sir.'

'Some might think you were trying it on.'

'Yes, sir. *They* might.'

I looked at his face on the screen. The image broke up and then came back again. He was on the move maybe. It was difficult to read his expression; he'd chosen to leave the metal plate surrounding his right eye-socket exposed. There was a long silence. Then, finally, he said: 'OK. I'll authorise it. But if you don't deliver this time, you're in deep.'

'Thank you, sir,' I said.

His image imploded and I sighed with relief. He obviously had other things on his mind. I *was* pushing my luck. (Sure I was). Mr. Al-Razzaq's intelligence had been useful when we nailed The Rotherhithe Corporation, but not essential by any means. I mailed the pharmacy at New Scotland Yard and a courier delivered the pills within an hour.

The first course compromised the efficiency of my thyroid gland, lowering my rate of metabolism to a crawl. (Within a week I would put on at least 70 pounds). The second course boosted my melanin production. A little baking under the sun-lamp was all it would take to turn my pale skin chocolate brown. I could manage the beard on my own.

As I turned into Mr. Al-Razzaq the others

217

gave me the usual crap in the canteen.

'Nice one, Proctor,' said Quinn. 'Getting paid for it again—with expenses. You've got some.'

I swallowed another dollop of LipoMax ice-cream and said nothing. It would only make things worse.

Mr. Al-Razzaq checked into the state registered brothel in Bermondsey Street at 2.00 am. As usual he had requested Cleo in advance. Cleo's standard peak-time charge was formidable, but then she was state-of-the-art. The consortium of pimp-surgeons who controlled the joint had grafted so much new muscle tissue into her vagina she was known to regulars as 'The Boa'. And if there was anybody in Bermondsey Street with the latest chemical accessories, it would be Cleo.

My While-U-Wait blood test was negative and I lost no time making conversation at the bar. I went straight to the elevator and punched in the basement code. The metal box began its creaky descent.

* * *

I was sitting naked on the four poster, looking over my monstrous stomach into her dark eyes. She would have been attractive without enhancement—but with it, she was devastating. In my best Etonian accent I said: 'I've heard there's something new around? For

218

the discerning client.'

'Where did you hear that?' She said, kissing my thigh and sending pulses of pleasure through my body.

'A man in my position . . .' I said, trailing off as if no more needed to be said.

She smiled but didn't elaborate.

'One of my aides called it—let me see now—Xanth?'

She raised her head and I reached down to lift her chin.

'Well?'

Her lacquered hair had been sculpted into a mane of purple and gold.

'It'll cost you.'

'Of course. How much?'

'Five hundred.'

I laughed out loud.

'Nothing's that good, surely.'

'Oh, yeah?'

She sounded confident.

'You'd recommend it?'

'Yes. No question.'

I thought for a moment. Would the Chief wear this? Well, I thought, he'll have to.

'I take it payment would not be made through the house?'

'No,' said Cleo. 'This would be a private arrangement.'

'I see.'

She stood aside while I heaved my bulk off the bed. I lumbered over to the chez and took

219

my wallet from the back pocket of my trousers. Taking out an impressive looking wad I peeled-off ten fifties—deliberately.

'Leave it on the dressing table.'

Cleo went into the bathroom and came out with a small bottle. She tipped the contents onto the glass surface of the bedside cabinet—a pile of fine, yellow crystals—and cut a line with a razor. She then produced a rolled up note and leaned forward.

'Hey,' I said. 'I thought this was for me?'

'It is,' she said.

'Then why are—'

She pushed me back down on the bed.

'Relax. You won't be disappointed.'

Cleo snorted the line up her nose and then held her breath for a few moments. Her breasts rose as her lungs filled with air.

'So?' I said.

She came towards me and I prepared to kiss her collagen packed lips; however, before my mouth met her hers, she exhaled in my face. *Ahh*, I thought, *the breathing thing*. I was vaguely aware of a slightly acrid smell before my brain ignited and I stumbled into paradise.

The next day, I sat at home trying to make sense of what had happened. My head didn't dock with reality until late afternoon—at least. Xanth was something else; a swift acting hallucinogen that transformed every sensation into an explosion of pleasure. Cleo's kisses; the colour red; the intoxicating smell of her perfume. Experience became symphonic. When she whispered her whore's patter next to my ear it was like a seraphim had dropped from God's hospitality suite—just to talk dirty.

*　　　*　　　*

I filed a report to the Chief and recommended we tail Cleo. After two weeks of observation— during which she spent most of her free hours at a local gym or shopping over the river— Quinn clocked two trips to a residential development on the Marshalsea Road. We were unfamiliar with the address, but realised we were on the right track when Still Life paid a call. Cooper brought him in for questioning.

Still Life looked as though he had just crawled out of an open grave. His complexion was pale but with a greenish bloom suggesting that he was in the early stages of purification. Once, he held the post of senior lecturer in neurochemistry at King's College. But that was ancient history. He had been dismissed for using the lab as a factory. Now he eked out a living as a dealer in the enterprise zone, funding his own terminal habit on the substantial proceeds of his trade.

He was carrying 5 grams of Xanth but refused to spill. He denied getting his Xanth from the Marshalsea address and claimed that he was just visiting a friend.

'You?' I said. 'Have friends?'

'Yes,' he replied, closing his heavy eyelids (both of which seemed to be coated with a dot-matrix pattern of fungal spores).

'What's his name?'

'Her name.'

'OK. Her name?'

'Joanna.'

Still Life wasn't very forthcoming. So, we put him in the fridge. He mumbled something about rights and wanting to contact his solicitor, Roger Partridge (a well known alcoholic and legal has-been), but we laughed in his face and gave him a bottle of Metropolitan H-syrup to keep him quiet. He was very grateful.

I dropped a gram of Xanth into the mini-lab and left it for an hour. When I came back the results showed that the key ingredient was a compound that bore a marked structural resemblance to lysergic acid diethylamide. Xanth also contained another highly complex haemoglobin-type substance. The rest was a curious amalgam of elements and bio-junk: copper, traces of chloride, catecholamines and some sex hormones.

When Joanna Stark finally emerged from her Marshalsea hideout she wasn't what we expected. Although still young—a teenager I guessed, she dressed at least two decades above her age. Frumpy. Conservative. Moreover, her Sunday morning jaunt took her only as far as the (anti-Islamic) Judaeo-

222

Christian Reform Church on Borough High Street. This was obviously her cover.

Toole and Kapur tracked her for a fortnight and she only went out three times. Twice to the church on Borough High Street and once to the Bill Gates Centre in Crucifix Street (where she was a volunteer at the soup kitchen for licensed beggars and asylum seekers).

At home, Holy Jo received two visits from dealers operating outside the enterprise zone: Marcus Elijah from Brixtonia and Tzu Kung from China Town. So obviously the word was out and travelling fast. We didn't intercept. We wanted surprise on our side. Nevertheless, we did stop and search three late callers (media from Soho)—all carrying Xanth. None of them would admit to buying their 'Yellow' from Joanna Stark. They said they had gone to see her for spiritual guidance (which was rich, especially coming from the one who imported Paedo-Snuff from Poland). Anyway, we locked them up with Still Life and raided the Marshalsea address the following morning before sun-up. We hauled a sleepy Holy Jo in for questioning and set the forensic boys loose in her modestly furnished home. Should have been easy. Boil in a bag. But by lunch time I knew we had problems.

Joanna Stark had the patience of a saint. She denied involvement in illicits and claimed that the people who visited her only did so for pastoral counselling. She drew attention to her

223

work at the Bill Gates Centre and asked me to contact the Rabbinate of the Judaeo-Christian Church on Borough High Street.

We ran a routine search on her ID, just for the hell of it. The net and official record sites are so hacked-up and infected, no one takes electronic evidence seriously any more. Nevertheless, we did our stuff to keep up appearances and hey, guess what? Her story squared.

Age nineteen. Born in Essex. Father— Professor Nils Stark (Cantab), recently deceased. Mother—Dorothea Stark, moved to Spain to live with her sister (after husband's death). Judaeo-Christian church records showed registration in several congregations: Brighton, Camberwell and the 17th arrondissement in Paris, and so on. It could have all been planted yesterday for all I knew. I tried to contact Joanna's mother, but the satellite was down (but even if I had got through, I might have spoken to an AI plant. Any Off-the-shelf system can jump the Turing hurdle these days).

Her While-U-Wait blood test was completely negative. Clean as a whistle. And the forensic boys couldn't find anything either. No factory apparatus at all. No condensers, burners, filters, test tubes. No rubber lines, no licensed drugs, no manuals. Nothing. And it got worse. No traces of illicits were found anywhere. Not even in the carpet.

'OK, Jo.' I said to her, aiming a hot beam of lamplight into her eyes. 'Where do you keep your rig?'

'What rig?'

'The factory.'

'What factory?'

'The Xanth factory? Where is it?'

'I'm sorry, I don't know what you're talking about.'

She toyed with a silver Star of David that hung around her neck and pressed her thumb against the Cross in it's centre.

'Inspector,' she said, looking into the blazing light. 'I'm telling you the truth.'

I figured that making her spend a night with our most recent guest (a lesbian psycho that Toole and Kapur had just brought in) might help matters. Kelsey was the business. So many steroids she was built like an ox: shaved head, studs, neo-nazi tattoos. The lot. The kind of girl you wouldn't want to take on without the aid of a stun-club.

'These cells don't have surveillance cameras?' Said Holy Jo, looking up at the empty corners and spider webs.

'That's right.' I said. 'We like to respect people's privacy.'

'You can't do this,' she said.

'Can't I?'

Kelsey stood up, flicked her Metropolitan Lebanese at the wall and licked her lips.

I had expected Holy Jo to start squealing at

this point. But she didn't. Just walked into the lion's den. That's the trouble with religious fanatics, they can't be trusted to behave normally. But then, as I got into the lift, I thought to myself: *But it's a cover, isn't it?*

*   *   *

Next morning I checked and asked the duty officer if there had been any action during the night.

'Kelsey made a bit of noise.'

'How do you mean?'

'Moans, cries. That sort of thing.'

'So? What did you do?'

'Went down. When I switched the light on she was in her bunk. Just moaning and writhing around.'

'What about Holy Jo?'

'Asleep.'

I shrugged and went into the conference room. By half nine all the team had arrived. Cooper, Toole, Kapur, Quinn, and two of the forensic boys. At the end of the meeting we all agreed that we had a big, big problem. The facts just didn't add up. One, punters were clearly collecting Xanth from Joanna Stark's Marshelsea residence and two, there wasn't a single piece of factory apparatus in there.

'Clearly, you've arrested the wrong person?' Said the senior forensic officer.

'Impossible,' I said. 'Everybody who calls on

her leaves with a sachet of Xanth.'

'But there's no factory.'

'It must be hidden. There's a false wall in there . . . or something.'

'We used the portable x-ray. What are you suggesting? A technical error?'

'Maybe.'

'The machine's a series 200. No chance.'

I was getting irritated.

'Boss,' said Toole. 'We really can't hold her. You're going to have to let her go.'

Joanna Stark was released at 10.34 am. I was gutted.

I started preparing a report for the Chief but couldn't finish it. I felt like I was typing my own death warrant. So, I gave up and took the lift down to see Kelsey.

She was still lying on her bunk with a dumb grin on her face.

'Hey, Kelsey?' I said. 'Good night?'

'Beautiful,' she said. 'Oh, just so beautiful.' There was something awfully familiar about her expression—that look of rapture.

In the corner of the room was a coffee mug with a tea spoon standing up inside it. Next to the mug was an ordinary cigarette lighter. I picked up the spoon and noticed the underside was still blackened.

I shook Kelsey and she opened her eyes.

'So beautiful.'

'Was it Xanth?' I asked. 'Was it?'

'What?'

227

'Was it Xanth—Gold, Yellow? Was it?'
'Yellow—sure it was. Cheers, Proctor.'
'But she was clean? How?'
Kelsey rolled over smiling.

I mobilised the crash team. But of course, Stark never went back to her flat. And of course, we never saw her again.

When Kelsey surfaced we agreed not to press charges if she told us how it was done. It was so simple. The colour should have given it away. All Stark needed was a supply of drinking water a teaspoon and a naked flame. She *was* the factory. An exquisite piece of genetic engineering. Glass tubes had been replaced by arteries; condensers and burners by kidneys and lungs. Maybe she had the genes spliced in, or maybe she was born like it. Whatever, her capacity to produce Xanth was probably as heritable as eye-colour.

I could see decades of legal wrangling ahead. This one would run and run. Home secretaries, human rights lawyers, activists, and gangsters. There was something in this for everyone.

I have the distinction of being the first law enforcement officer to describe a human factory in an official report. When the Metropolitan drugs Tzar read it, he resigned. He could see the writing was on the wall—in bright, bright yellow.

The Black Box

Tonino Benacquista
Translated by Melanie Laurent

There was this great ray of white light. I felt my body rising up in the darkness at an incredible speed and was scared of crashing into an invisible boundary to the cosmos. A warm breeze brought me back to Earth, laying me down in the middle of a fearful land. Motionless and unable to rise to my feet or even to open my eyes, all I could do was listen. There were howling dogs and starving wolves, wounded hyenas with shrill laughter and big cats growling around my carcass. Silence and oblivion took centuries to weave a cocoon, in which I eventually curled up.

Until a merciful God gave me back my sight.

And my life.

*   *   *

A woman let out a sigh of relief as I regained consciousness. I thought she was a mother or a sister. It was the nurse.

No headache or particular anxiety. They must have pumped my veins with morphine or something. She tells me about an accident, and

229

immediately I have the headlights of the car in my eyes. The shock wave that followed still resonates through my backbone. And then nothing. I ask her how long that *nothing* lasted for. One night? Only one night? I feel like I have travelled backwards across eternity in a mere twelve hours. Where must those who spend a year in a coma go?

My father asked to be rung as soon as I awoke. I do not want him to come all the way out here but I've no intention of being stranded here, in a hospital in the Pyrenees. The doctor must call and reassure me about my progress. In a few days I will become myself again. In a few years I will remember this accident as a vague black hole followed by a short and never-ending stay in a white bed surrounded by snow, stretching as far as the eye can see.

The car was a BMW. No one could have done anything for the driver. I honestly believe I was careful. The nurse confirms this in her own way; no one in the area has ever seen a vehicle taking the Goules road at such speed.

'Do we know who this guy is?'

'Someone working for an insurance company based in Limoges. The autopsy will show he was drunk, you can bet on that!'

I feel a lot better. A drunkard nearly cost me my life and I thanked God not to have his death on my conscience. The great reaper turns minds inside out. I must concentrate all my energy on this new life; after all, it's not everyday you're resuscitated. They say those who've faced death spend the rest of their existence in serenity and joy. If this is the case, maybe it was worth it.

The nurse behaves strangely, she rushes around my bed staring at me, half amused and half intrigued. As if I was a celebrity. This accident did not make me amnesic though. My name is Laurent Aubier and I am thirty-five. I repair photocopiers, I'm single and my great ambition is to win the Lepine Prize, for the best inventor in France. The woman in white confirms these facts with a knowing smile. It's as if she's aware of every last detail of my life. This annoys me a little, so I tell her.

'Perhaps, I know a lot more about you than you do.' She answers, leaving the room.

*   *   *

I phoned and reassured all those who'd inquired after me. I never knew I had so many friends and relatives. Usually they only talk to me to get free photocopies. The nurse brings me my dinner. How can they promote the idea of a 'hospital with a friendly face' when they serve food that Amnesty International would condemn? I call the nurse later this evening. She comes and clears out the pisspot, which had started to irritate me. I hate sharing such intimacy with a woman I don't know; as anyone confined to a bed must do. My own mother never saw this much of me when she was alive; and back in Paris the girlfriends that came and went never so much as heard me sneeze.

'Don't watch TV too late, otherwise I'll have to come back and switch it off for you.'

'You take your job too seriously Mrs . . . Mrs?'

'Janine.'

'Thank you for everything you've done here, Mrs Janine, but TV will send me to sleep a lot faster than your pills. And anyway it seems like I've had enough sleep to last ten years.'

She tells me off playfully and I thank her with a smile. I suddenly realise that the nice lady has been working around me since this morning, on her own and without a break.

'I watched over you all last night, while you were in your coma. This is a small hospital, Mr Aubier; one of my colleagues is off sick and the other is on holiday. I'll try to catch a few hours sleep, providing you're quieter than you were last night . . . '

I didn't have time to ask what she meant; she winked mischievously and left. As far as I can remember, no one ever commented on me sleep talking; neither at boarding school nor at my flat (where I often brought home beautiful insomniacs). My nightmares probably came one after the other during those horrible, missing hours. They watch over the coma patients so they don't toss and turn. I generally remember my dreams, in which angst, gory movies and Buñuelian symbolism mix happily together. Janine must have heard a lot of stories. Unless all I did was go over and over the accident, groaning menacingly at each moment of impact. I must forget this soon. The TV schedule I've just devised for myself is undoubtedly going to help: a Jerry Lewis movie, a documentary about the Komodo Dragon and to finish off, a repeat from last year's Bayreuth Festival. If my calculations are correct Visconti's *Ludwig* will end just as Janine comes in with my breakfast. Life is too short and too precious to spend sleeping.

*   *   *

'It still smells of tobacco in here.'

'Fuck. When will I get out of here?'

'Tonight, I've told you a hundred times. But, if you insist on fidgeting, we could keep you here a little longer.'

Fresh-faced and rested—little Janine. I would not be surprised if she had put a bit of make up on. Since my first day here I have seen Marielle, Bernadette, Sylvie and Mrs Beranger. They are all lovelier than they know, but no one could steal Janine's crown.

'What's your husband like?'

'Oh, Mr Aubier you're so nosy.'

233

'Come on . . . '

'You must have someone, right?'

She blushes only slightly.

'He's less rowdy than you.'

'Janine . . . (I lower my voice) I hear nurses are always naked under their dresses.'

She shrugs her shoulders, and fluffs a pillow before replacing it behind my head.

'That can remain a fantasy, if you don't mind. Keep it with the others you're hoarding.'

'What do you mean by that?'

'What would your Betty have to say if she could hear you now?'

'Betty?'

'I won't be here today, but I'll come and say goodbye before you leave.'

'Don't do that to me! Betty who?'

'You were asking for it, Mr Aubier. Have a nice day all the same.'

'Janine come back here, *immediately*!'

The bitch!

She did not come to see me today. Searching for Janine throughout the hospital, I realised how frail I was. Betty . . . Did I talk about a Betty in my sleep? I don't know anyone called Betty.

Or maybe I do.

But it seems so far away . . .

A school desk for two, the kind that no longer exists. An inkwell in each corner, which the mistress would come round and refill from a bottle. A small trap door opens far away in my memory. I had carved *Bety* in the wood with my Sergeant Major quill's nib. She mocked me and I added a 't' close to the first one. I remember now . . . her white teeth . . . her eyes unbelievably pure . . . the rustling of our overalls as our elbows brushed. They called us lovers more than once. I remember our eyes meeting across the hall every morning. 'What's your girlfriend called?' 'Betty!' To the same question she would answer 'Laurent'.

I don't know if I've truly been in love since.

The night falls. I put my razor in a side pocket of my suitcase. I have not stopped looking for those sweet memories all day long. Walking through the hospital, I still picture that little girl's smile.

I am ready to step back into the world, though it hasn't missed me that much during the last ten days. Bernadette and Sylvie are at the reception desk. I promise myself I'll send them something from Paris. Janine arrives in her weekend clothes. She beckons me over to the huge red chairs of the waiting room where no one's waiting.

'Your taxi won't be long now.'

'With a bit of luck, it will be late. I haven't thanked you yet for everything you've done.'

'That's just part of my job.'

'Thanks to you I recalled a childhood sweetheart. She was in there, hidden deep, and without you she would never have re-surfaced.

It's to you I owe these bubbles of nostalgia.'

She lets out a short laugh but quickly regains her calm. A flash of seriousness passes through her eyes. She hesitates, not daring to continue. So much so I stop smiling, as does she.

'You remember I watched over you while you were in a coma, Mr Aubier?'

'Yes, you told me after.'

'You were in what's called a "vigilant coma". It's a rather light coma. The patient expresses himself, reacts and mutters an incomprehensible stream of sentences throughout. It can last for hours on end. It's a state of organised delirium that only the patients themselves can understand. Most of the time even they can't comprehend half of it. Ten hours . . . Do you realise? Ten hours of verbal delirium without a single interruption.'

'. . . ?'

'This is a great chance, Mr Aubier. An opportunity not to be missed. An antenna receiving all the elements of your black box.'

'My black box?'

'The unconscious, if you prefer, Mr Aubier.'

Janine appeared in a new light before my timid eyes. A passionate and nervous being: half priestess, half witch.

'That night you told your own life story. You went to the end of your limits and distilled thirty-five years of morals, taboos and memories. You dusted them down, ironed them out, decoded and rearranged them in an

236

order only known to you. Betty is just a drop in the ocean, she came out of the black box, like so many others.'

A stab of fear pierces my stomach. Hot blood rushes through my arms and back. I see the taxi's light appear in the window.

'Janine . . . You're telling me that you . . . invaded my privacy?'

She takes my hands and squeezes them.

'Laurent, I started to see an analyst fourteen years ago. In those fourteen years, I've uttered only half of what you said in one night.'

She holds up a spiral notebook. I start to think I'm going crazy.

'For once the nightshift was rather quiet, and I have this habit of taking notes . . . '

The book lands in my hand and my head is a blur. The taxi honks.

'You're having a laugh?'

'It was a favour. I did you a favour. I'd like to think somebody would do the same for me, in similar circumstances. All your mysteries, loves, hatreds, fears, fantasies, everything that you forgot and all the messages that didn't get through to you are written down here. Put it to good use.'

I want to grab her by the arm but she escapes, disappearing into the changing rooms. The taxi is about to leave.

I stay there, unable to make a decision, like a idiot.

237

I didn't dare open it until I got on the plane. The air hostess poured me a generous glass of wine while the person next to me thought it would be useful to explain that a fear of flying usually covered up other things, like the fear of leaving or the fear of change. Another fool who wants to stick his nose into my business. The pages Janine scrawled are more dangerous than any phobia. I could rip them into small pieces and flush them down the toilet; no one would know anything about it and I could go on living as if nothing happened. My life is ordinary and I like it that way; I don't need to understand all its secrets. What's the point in exploring a no-go area? Everybody knows all I'll find is trouble; it's the moral of any movie that's ever been set in the jungle. What's the point in studying the mechanics of the soul? *I did you a favour . . .* What a favour, my sweet Janine. Who wants to understand what happens on the other side? Who isn't scared of the trapdoor that opens to the ego? I'm sure it doesn't smell too good in there. *Put it to good use . . .* what if I had more to lose than win in this story?

But the question is how can I resist?

My neighbour has dozed off, his skull against the window.

I lift open the book's tan cover.

*   *   *

. . . We should go back there, to the old Smackhard's house, we might find his saving book there, oh yeah! (Laughter) . . . Ten years of drinking tonic is bound to leave some trace, isn't it, Nathalie . . . ? Everything was even whiter under his robe, it was so white and painful to look at, lost in this great white, white cone, it was this fucker Pascal who made me . . . The bells and everything . . . he did not get it, old Pascal . . . 'My sister loves money too much, my sister loves money too much' That's all you ever said, dick head . . . You didn't go there, you never went under the great white cone . . .

*   *   *

'Shall I take you to the bathroom?'

The hostess puts her hand on my shoulder. She removes a white bag, lost between the brochures and magazines in the seat pocket, offering it me in case I need to vomit. She would rather I did it in the bathroom. Do I look as bad as I feel? She hands me a tablet and some water. I swallow both. Obedient. I force myself to smile so she goes away. Janine is a funny bitch. She shouldn't have done that. Her duty that night was to close the door and respect the privacy of my thoughts, let them be lost in the universe's great unconscious. I close my eyes and take a long breath before I set out to look for *the great white cone*. It must be somewhere so far and so near, lost along the way, forgotten for a long time but still just as white. What was hiding under *the great white cone* . . .? It is here, very close. Very close . . .

'Excuse me, you dropped your notebook.'

'. . . Uh?'

I thank the fool, with a nod and pick up the book, which fell to my feet. *The great white cone* should not be much further. Never mind, I'll return to it when I'm alone. There are forty-eight pages of crowded notes with a series of repetitions annotated. I don't know whether to read from cover to cover or just dip in. I light a cigarette, unable to resist although understanding that it is now forbidden.

*   *   *

. . . I have cried, fuck, everyone saw me. I don't want to be called Roland, my name is Laurent, not Roland, Lau-rent, like Lorenzaccio. Fucking hell! He was tall and thin though, thin alright, the dick, but mostly tall, and I was scared because he had the law on his side . . . You always liked to take the piss out of people, there would always be someone who would get back at you . . . His initials written with a branding iron on my pride . . . A . L . . . Auguste Lespinasse . . . You bet I made up some shit about Auguste Lespinasse . . . It was a delight . . . My name is Laurent, Lau-rent, got it . . . ?

A tall guy with glasses. The national service in Montbeliard. Humiliated before the whole dormitory. I pushed it a bit too far. Stupid puns on his name, nobody had laughed at them and for this I was punched in the face. Everything comes back to me; the furrow of the tears on my cheeks and the metal bridge on the right side of his mouth. As a punishment he called me Roland until the end of my military service. Each night, like a coward, I dreamt of killing him in his sleep.

This episode was not forgotten but I could not imagine how deeply it had affected me. Since that day I have never once tried to hurt another person and maybe I owe this to Auguste Lespinasse. The fear that comes from holding these incendiary pages is becoming more intense and more exhilarating. What if Janine was right? What if she had given me the key to *knowledge*, to the most crucial knowledge of all, the understanding of oneself? This may be a treasure, lying on my lap, like a small Pandora's box. It could answer the essential questions, the ones, which they say belong to us when death looms. It will tell me who I am and where I come from. And maybe I will get the chance to know where I am heading. Half-way through my life. Long before my time is done.

The hostess asks me to put out my cigarette. I light another one as soon as she is gone. I defy what's forbidden, I am too old and I don't care. We are now flying above Paris. The guy next to me already has his hand on his brief case. I still have time for the soul-traversing index.

*   *   *

... *Hopeless!* ... *Hopeless!* ... *That's all she ever said, the old slut* ... *Dad, you must believe me, not her! I am not hopeless* ... *Don't play with your cars on the stairs!* ... *I don't want to repeat a year, she is a liar and you believe her!* ... *Be careful!* ... *godfather's big marble staircase* ... *Italian marble* ... *Hopeless! It's disgusting the very sound of it* ... *My head is full of sand* ... *Full of sand, eh, I will demonstrate some amateur acrobatics* ... *(drum roll with the tongue)* ... *The hopeless one will now perform the swan dive!* ... *Marble is beautiful, but cold* ...

*   *   *

I am in a taxi but do not how I got here and have no recollection of landing or picking up my suitcase. It's like I am still in the air. Almost weightless. Until now the only picture I associated with that fall was a surgical collar, which made me look like a little old man. I was

242

six. The staircase could have cost me my life. Who was this old slut? What does she have to do with the fall? A pile of mail awaits me behind the door. I rush to the phone, not even taking off my coat.

'Dad?'

'Son, you're back? I could have collected you from the airport.'

'You remember my fall, on godfather's staircase?'

'Do I remember? Your mother and I thought you were dead.'

'What happened to me at school that year?'

'. . . ?'

'I need to know. You always kept an eye on me at school.'

'It's strange . . . Asking me this after such a long time. You were in reception when it happened. It was in May and you didn't return to school until September.'

'Did I repeat the year?'

'No, that's what your teacher wanted though, she was an old hag you always squabbled with. After your fall, we got you a private tutor until you were fully recovered. You were superior to many of your class mates when school started again.'

'How did I manage to fall down those stairs?'

'I don't know. We were all sat at the table then we heard you tumbling down the stairs and found you at the bottom, unconscious.

Your godfather was distraught.'

I thanked him a million times and hung up. Everything became clearer. The old hag hated me; to repeat a year would have been a death sentence.

I have heard it said that the very idea of suicide cannot form in a child's head. I have known the despair that leads one towards death. I was six years old.

*　　　*　　　*

I have not returned to work for three weeks. I have spent most of my time in the park or in my flat. My apparent inertia hides the extraordinary toil constantly taking place in my head. Beneath my skull is a storm so violent, it drags with it torrents of forgotten promises and unsuspected taboos. I remain hunched over the notebook like somebody studying a treasure map. I dive in like a deep sea explorer and rise to the surface only after a painful ordeal. A lot of things still elude me within the notebook, and the opaque elements are those which I find most intriguing.

*　　　*　　　*

When I am old, I will be a spaghetti farmer, that is a great job . . . When I am old, I will be a spaghetti farmer, that is a great job . . . Acquisition of Fin Oil by the AC Group before

244

March . . . When I am old, I will be a spaghetti farmer, that is a great job . . .

* * *

Spaghetti farmer. With big efforts, I pictured this tall dickhead, Pascal, in the nursery school, as he explained that pasta was harvested in fields, just like wheat. On the other hand, it is impossible to find where this Fin Oil popped up from. My friend Jeremy is a small time speculator. He explained to me that a small company like the AC Group could never afford Europe's biggest oil trust. The worst is how these two words slipped inside my mind and stayed there, sticking to each other like limpets. Is our cortex filled with millions of insignificant things stocked up through the ages? There is surely something worth searching for behind the riddle. I am unable to crack the code. Some paragraphs are disconcerting, especially when they are expressing the exact opposite of my conscious thoughts.

* * *

. . . One should never betray a friend, you bastard . . . We were like Riri, Fifi and Loulou . . . Ask Judas! How many games of pinball for God's sake! . . . My poor Richard . . . Did you like little Sophie that much? Why didn't you tell

me, you fucker . . . all those games of pinball to end up here . . .

* * *

Fifi was Phillipe, Riri was Richard and Loulou was me. The trio. Always hanging out together in high school. I was quick to be accepted into their gang. Phillipe liked me especially. I have heard that women pay so much attention to detail that they can hide their lovers for years, and detect a mistress from a single hair. In my case the opposite was true. After an eight-day course in Toulouse, I found a Romeo y Julieta stub in the ashtray on our night table; the same kind of cigar I gave to Phillipe. The box of twenty-five cost me a fortune, but money is nothing when it comes to a mate's birthday. I never forgave Sophie or that bastard. That was ten years ago.

The trouble is, the black box tells a different story.

I cannot see how it could be better informed than me. It's written here, in black and white, by Janine's nervous hand: *My poor Richard . . . Did you like little Sophie that much?* Janine might have been wrong after all. Names were uttered in a whirlwind of words. Richard, my very old friend, unfailing Richard. I do not want my unconscious to suggest this; the whole story was painful enough then.

I had to be clear in my mind about it.

246

The waitress puts two coffees on the table, and I light this dinner's first cigarette. Richard takes a cigar out of its case without stopping his brilliant analysis of the bullet proof invincibility of the middle classes.

'Was it Phillipe who introduced you to cigars?'

He pauses and looks at me surprised.

'It's been a while since you've mentioned him. I thought you never wanted to hear his name again.'

'Time has passed . . . Ten? Twelve years? You live and forget, I suppose. I managed to forget Sophie when I never thought I would.'

'Some things can not be forgiven.'

'I'm not talking about forgiveness; everybody has their own take on morals. Our mental health depends on how we obliterate troublesome memories. Borges wrote beautifully on the subject. Let's imagine we all have a vessel within our self, keeping record of the best and worst, especially the worst.

'You mean like a black box, on a plane?'

'Exactly.'

Richard looks at me, motionless. Disturbed. Then he slowly lights a cigar, following a ritual I know well.

'Something's changed since your accident. We would never have talked about these things before.'

I maintain an ambiguous silence, as if to emphasise the strange direction of our conversation.

'If this box did exist, no one should have access to it,' he says. 'It's our doubts and mistakes that make us who we are. What could so many small certainties do for us?'

'They could help us understand how we became what we are.'

The waiter places the bill on the corner of the table, breaking an intense eye contact, which could have lasted hours.

'To answer your question, it's not Phillipe who introduced me to cigars, but you.'

'. . . Me?'

'You remember the Romeo y Julieta you got for him? He never dared telling you but the odour of cigars made him sick. I tasted one and it was a revelation. I smoked the whole box, and to this day the habit has cost me around a thousand euros a month.'

After a few seconds of silence, I let out a short laugh. An innocent laugh, that is neither bitter nor vengeful. The new intimacy I have with the black box must have changed me. How could I ever believe the box would be wrong? What we naively describe as 'reason' helps us believe what we want. The unconscious is full of relentless truths. Ten years ago I already *knew* that Richard and Sophie had slept together. We only fool ourselves. Through the years that followed I stayed friends with the traitor, always ignoring the innocent one . . .

Gradually, the café empties out. Richard leaves a large tip for the waiter. Probably so he will leave us alone for as long as possible. Neither of us have spoken for the last few minutes, yet never before have we talked so much. His black box must record a lot of information at top speed. These machines are ultra efficient.

How intense are the moments when words become meaningless? They bring things to a beautiful close.

'What I don't understand is why the dickhead Phillipe didn't react when I called him a bastard?'

His smile lacked the sarcasm I expected. A smile of nostalgia, perhaps.

'Phillipe was trapped in a Cornelian Choice. He could either vindicate himself or betray me. He preferred to take the blame.'

'To be that nice borders on stupidity, doesn't it, Richard?'

'. . . Who knows?'

He gets up and puts his coat on, a cigar between his lips. We shake hands on the restaurant doorstep.

'I'll pay next time.'

'Okay.'

*   *   *

249

We often wonder what we would do, given the chance to know our own future. Now I understand the knowledge of the past is more extraordinary. To fear the future is nothing in comparison with the fear of the past. The future is nothing but a late realisation of the past.

At this point, I have not been to work for two months. The doctor believed my stories: dizziness, headaches, troubled sleep and exhaustion; all this happened after my terrible accident.

I was given a few more weeks off, and my boss couldn't say anything about it. Someone from the Lepine Prize Committee phoned me to say I stood a good chance of winning and I pretended to be flattered. If only they knew I had become hooked on a hard drug. A junkie; that's what I am. Addicted to my own psyche and desperate to free my confined self. Fascinated by the number of revelations I'd received into my own, strange personality. And I want more, always more, like all junkies. I know the forty-eight pages practically by heart. At times I recite extracts, as I must have done in the coma while Janine watched over me. A victim of a despicable copulation between my id and superego. Certain mysteries resolve themselves but others refuse to become explained, some formulas remain obscure sending me into a powerless state of rage. I have managed to isolate around thirty sentences, thirty riddles. Some of these make me scream with anger.

*   *   *

. . . *My poor Mr Vernier, this will be played at the finishing line, but I am already the winner* . . .
. . . *Put together, those two were like* The Luncheon on the Grass *and* The Andalusian Bitch.
. . . *I can picture Bertrand, majestic and plump, with a small glass ball on his belly! What an actor!*
. . . *One must enlarge the life thing six times, that is the secret* . . .

*   *   *

And there are many other inexplicable memories. I do not recognise any names or situations and this creates a haunting emptiness, a need to know. Suddenly the phone rings, bringing me back to the present. I snatch the receiver, cursing whoever's interrupting my thoughts.
'How did you know?'
'Jeremy?'
'Damn, how did you know?'
'What?'
'The AC Group made the acquisition of Fin Oil for God's sake!'

251

' . . . ?'

'A lightning bolt! A bolt from the blue! Who gave you this tip?'

'I don't know.'

'Are you taking the piss? If I could have believed that was possible, I would be a billionaire by now.'

'I don't know Fin Oil from Adam. Are they really that big?'

'Big? It's not even just a holding company; it's like a stock market in itself. It has tentacles spreading through all industries, food processing, computing, everywhere and more subsidiaries than it can care for. Comeco and Soparep belong to them, so does the N.W.D and the . . . '

The National Ware Distribution! I go there every two weeks to look after their eighty photocopiers. I probably printed out this detail without realising it, a small detail ignored by my brain but recorded onto the black box. Jeremy does not believe me when I tell him that I don't know anything. What's the point in explaining the story of the notebook? If I told him about Janine's psychotherapy and the great white cone, he would think I was going crazy. Which I surely am. I asked my colleague Pierrot to search through the files in the department, and see when the last time I visited National Ware Distribution was. Last July I had to repair six photocopiers, including one in the manager's office. The secretary's face quickly came back to me; a brown haired girl with luscious eyes, who was moaning about the fact that both the photocopier and the coffee machine had broken down on the same day. When I opened the machine, I detected the most common problem and was able to fix it inside ten minutes. As I always do when paper gets jammed in the system, I glanced at the sheet before throwing it in the bin. It was certainly here that I read this confidential letter and became aware of the AC Group making the acquisition of Fin Oil. A simple sentence, which would have evaporated in the mist of my brain without the black box.

But for one measly victory I suffer a thousand oppressive defeats, each one eating me alive. What remains of my senses urges me to give up this search, but a submerged voice drives me on. I want to know who the Andalusian bitch is and *Mr Vernier* too; he is mentioned seven times in the forty-eight pages. I want to know what the *life thing* is. And all the rest, all the absurd but meaningful jumble.

I want to know everything.

Everything.

*   *   *

I have started to write down my dreams six or seven times a night. Time does not exist for junkies. Unfortunately, the morning's harvest is always the same. Dreams emanate from the unconscious but are contaminated with the nonsense of daily life, and as a whole they seem to have a gratuitous nature. And yet I need a secure and direct way to channel the black box again.

I re-read Aldous Huxley's *Doors of Perception*. This guy must have been equally hooked on the black box. He goes as far as to recommend the use of bizarre substances to open it. Having no habit of consuming such substances, I asked Pierrot (who regularly smokes joints, locked in the toilet of our workshop) to find everything he can get his hands on; so I can dig a tunnel to my most secret self. The results of the experiment were particularly disappointing. The several joints knocked me out for hours on the sofa, bringing a thirty-five ton weight on each knee. The lines of coke ('80% pure' according to Pierrot) provoked an uncontrollable urge to do the housework; I hoovered and polished the silverware until four a.m. while developing a theory, which disproved both Newton and Copernicus. Opium did nothing for me; reading *Tintin and the Blue Lotus* again would have been more spectacular. I finished stylishly by dropping a tab of LSD, which made me do stupid things like fighting a 3D roman legion and calculating the precise amount of hydrogen molecules in my bath. I bear no grudge against Pierrot or Huxley. I know I am hunting a white whale, one that's drifting through the pit of my bowels.

*   *   *

'Mr Aubier, would you follow me please.'

When I entered the hypnotist's cabinet, I thought I would find trinkets but I saw only an armchair, on which I sat. I didn't know how to answer the question 'What can I do for you?' All I gave him was a list of proper nouns and sentences, asking him to mention them during the session. I secretly hoped one of them would provoke a reaction. Slightly disconcerted by the list, he explained the scientific principles of his work in a rational way, but I was not interested.

'We can try, but what you're asking is impossible. Have you tried to see an analyst? I could give you some addresses.'

'An analyst? You probably won't believe me when I tell you I already know everything about my father, my mother, my formative moments and libido. That is quite enough for me. I want to understand who Mr Vernier and the others are. Do you think this could be done in twenty years of psychotherapy?'

The following quarter of an hour was a peaceful and pleasant experience. Half asleep in a big armchair, I felt good and was able to empty my mind for a while.

'I am sorry Mr Aubier. You are a very

receptive subject but what you describe as your black box refused to open. Let me know if you ever succeed in opening it.'

While he was showing me the door, I absently got out my packet of Gitanes. I put a cigarette to my lips and something strange happened; I started to gag.

'One detail, Mr Aubier. As soon as you opened your mouth, it was like being next to an ashtray. I said a few words to your black box while you were under hypnosis. You have not completely wasted your time.'

*   *   *

I searched so desperately for myself I turned into somebody else. I policed my soul, or worse, became a private detective who would never finish his investigation. My memories are merely wild dreams and my future, a nightmare. Sometimes I wake up terrified with a picture in my head: the black box being struck repeatedly with a chisel until it opens. It is battered and bleeds but nothing comes out. I did not deserve this, my poor Janine. After all, I was only somebody who fixed photocopiers. I say 'was' because I lost my job. Even Pierrot grew tired of my absurd questions (did I ever tell you about *an Andalusian bitch*? Do you know Bertrand? He carries a *small glass ball on his belly.*) My father looks at me like I'm deranged, or worse, like a stranger using his own language (*Itchi Mitchi Bo*, did I say that when I was young?). Not knowing who Mr Vernier is will kill me. It's a shame. I started to like him. I made a little space for him in my head. Maybe it was somebody important, who will ever know?

This morning I received a letter informing me I had won the Lepine Prize. They will present it to me tomorrow in a ceremony for the opening of the Paris Fair. If only they knew how trivial this is to me now. The only intelligent invention would be a crocodile clip connecting the black box to a twelve-inch monitor. Maybe one day I will create a prototype. I have the rest of my life for this.

*   *   *

I went there like one goes to the dentist, dragging myself with no hope of having a good time. The crowd, the onlookers, the stalls and the speech; I had waited for this moment for months but today was just a lot of hot air, an empty ritual. I am far away from all this. I have a great white cone in my head.

'The winner is Mr Laurent Aubier and his Polaroid photocopier!'

Applause. The smoke bothers me. The noise bothers me even more. Pierrot deserves this prize as much as me; we knocked this device up together in our free time in the workshop. Like anyone working in an office, we photocopied parts of our bodies so much so we came up with the idea of combining the machine with an instant film case. A simple gadget I managed to optimise by improving the snapshot quality and its infinite duplication. The applications are incredible; they go from technical drawing to office automation right through to marketing and even contemporary art. Pierrot convinced me to enter the competition. They handed the prize to me, patted me on the back and silenced the audience with a gesture.

'An honorary prize will be posthumously awarded to Mr Alain Vernier, who recently died in a tragic car accident. Some applause please.'

. . . Alain who?

'Mr Vernier' he went on 'was a regular in this competition. For years, he presented us with inventions, which are now part of everyday life. He had never won the first prize though. Let's honour his memory tonight.'

My legs are like cotton wool; I sit on top of a speaker. The audience scatters and spreads out into the Fair. I grab the presenter by the arm.

'Where did this accident happen?'

'In the Pyrenees, last October. No one knows what he was doing there. Mr Vernier worked for an insurance company and seldom left Limoges.

I do. I know what he was doing there.

That night on the Goules road, I was hunted. Both of us knew we were in the final. I did not attach importance to this. But to him, it had become an obsession.

Mr Vernier wanted the first prize; he wanted it bad. After so many years he wanted to win at all costs.

If he had managed to knock me into a ditch on that night, everyone would have believed it was an accident. And I would have too, without Janine and the black box.

After all, they only unlock it once the damage is done.

A Case of Identity

Michael Jecks

It had cost him a fortune, that passport. Not because it was illegal, but because his need was so obvious. Someone in his position couldn't afford to stay, not even when his wife and daughter remained. When the authorities were after you there was only limited time to escape; and the desperate have to pay.

He'd known he'd have to bolt when he realised he was being watched.

The farm had long been the centre of attention, and the dogs had patrolled his fences enthusiastically all through the hotter weather, their ridged backs terrifying his workers when they materialized from the bushes, heads lowered in truculent demonstration, brows wrinkled and glowering. Alan had loved those two, the dog and the bitch. When he found their corpses out by the boundary fence, even as he wept over them, he was reviewing his options. The two were proof that an attack would come soon.

The government didn't want his family. Others might—it was possible that they could be held and ransomed—but even here women and children tended to be safe. No, it was him they'd try to 'arrest'; *him* whom they would shoot and leave in a dirt track far from anyone. Not the dignity of a grave for someone who worked against this government.

He'd escape and go to England. Where people were free.

*   *   *

Paul Jeffries yawned and glanced across the Arrivals hall to Jeannie.

She was wearing her 'invisible' clothes today: grey trouser suit; a small briefcase of ballistic material holding her laptop hanging from her shoulder; dark hair bobbed in a vaguely professional cut; her face partly concealed behind small, rectangular glasses. But it couldn't hide her delicate bone structure. Like Michelle Pfeiffer, Paul reckoned. Really good-looking, but with a sort of healthiness about her. Pfeiffer was almost unwell-looking, with those big pale eyes and all. Jeannie was plain gorgeous once you noticed her—not that many did. She just blended into the background, the best of their intake.

He lifted a finger to his right eye and scratched at the eyebrow three times—'I need a pee'—saw her acknowledge tersely, and moved away from Arrivals to the toilets.

She was often short with him. Probably she'd guessed he was crap. She'd been with him almost from day one, and perhaps because she was so much older and more confident in herself, she resented his laziness and stupidity. That was his impression, anyway. Meanwhile, all he wanted to do was rip her clothes off and get sweaty with her.

It could just be the shift. Most hated this—first thing in the morning, keeping an eye on tourists, holidaymakers, businessmen, and Christ knew who else, but Paul liked it. He'd always wanted to make use of his degree, and although this wasn't the way he'd anticipated things panning out, with his good second in Anthropology and Psychology, he was happy enough. Standing about here, simply watching the folks walking back into the country was itself an education.

Sometimes the best part was watching the others who worked here. Especially cops. Jesus, he'd almost jumped a crew last month. He'd seen them shoving packets into pockets before walking to customs, and it was only when the first in the line had held up his warrant card at the gate that he'd realised they'd come over from Holland. There were enough who'd go there for a smoke, and these had brought back a small stash. Bleeding idiots, if you asked Paul. He'd never smoked, and didn't see why others should.

Jeannie smoked sometimes. It had been useful, when she'd been watching someone who was a smoker. There was a sort of fraternity among the morons. They'd stand and exchange sidelong, self-effacing grins;

rapport established without words. She'd been able to get closer to them by bringing out her own pack and apologetically nodding towards their lighter. Fluent in Arabic and Swahili, she'd been able to stand nearby and listen without their having the faintest idea. Not that many would look twice at her anyway. No one thought that a coloured woman would work for a disgraced government like this British one.

Yeah, she was a diamond among the watchers.

He washed his hands, fastidious to the last, left the toilets and strolled over to the concessions. Buying good filter coffee, he moved over to the farther side of the hall, from where he still had an unimpeded view of Jeannie.

'Hi, Pete! How's it hanging?'

'Dave. Nothing so far today.'

David was the massively ineffectual section head of the team. More proof of the rash of urgent recruiting and promotions in recent years, and the perfect example of the *Peter Principal*—once a moderately competent operative, as manager of the team he had reached his own level of incompetence. Soon it would be noticed, and another effective watcher would be removed from the field. Daft.

After 9/11, the British government had reversed decades of under-investment in immigration and customs controls, and started making changes. The disaster of 7/7 in London added urgency to the new policy. Where politicians had floundered ineffectually, the big guns of business took their opportunity.

Weapons and surveillance companies had suffered with the peace dividend after the Cold War, and turned their best sales teams onto the police and politicians. Police commanders keen to exercise more authority demanded better guns, more cameras, identity cards, new laws to ban everything from airguns to congregations larger than two people with a child; and a callow, incompetent government swallowed every worst-case scenario presented to them. The power to arrest and hold men and women, uncharged, returned for the first time in four hundred years.

With these came the need for accurate surveillance on the ground.

The Watchers had been all but disbanded under previous administrations, but suddenly they were needed. Once-redundant officers were offered new packages, tempted with golden hellos, but few wanted to return. Burned once, they were less eager for more. So Human Resources had to seek new blood, returning to the usual fertile grounds: the universities. Not only Oxbridge, either. The new government couldn't swallow that sort of injustice. The new world order demanded equality in controlling the public.

Yes, the services were taking on people from the smaller universities. The main thing was bodies on the streets and at ports. Which was how Paul had slipped in, really. And how David had been put in charge of his own team when he was scarcely able to use a phone, let alone the radios.

'We have a new one,' Dave was saying.

Paul took the file with surprise. It was not usual for his leader to present him with a file so conspicuously. Just as Paul was not allowed to have his earpiece plugged in, because the little clear plastic coil gave away his profession, all briefings were supposed to be given in the room out at the back, behind the Special Branch area. He glanced at it, and felt a little worm of anxiety moving in his belly. 'What is it?'

'FARC. Watch the BA flight from Bogotà. Twenty minutes.'

*　　　*　　　*

Andy Campbell was in the armoury already. His vest was itching, the heavy weight of the ceramic plates pulling at his shoulders as he pulled out the magazine from his H&K sub-machinegun, then drew back the cocking lever to empty the breech. The cartridge flew out, and he caught it with a practised snatch of his hand. He racked the breech a couple of times, from habit, pulled the trigger to ease the springs, and put the gun down on the table.

He wouldn't be here many more times. He'd been a specialist shooter here at the airport for some months, but he couldn't carry on. Not once he'd admitted what had happened.

It was last night. He'd knocked off bloody late after doing a favour and working a shift at Heathrow because they'd had a minor flu epidemic. Jack, his partner, and he'd taken overtime and given them a hand, but he'd known he had to be up at four to get to Gatwick airport for the first shift. He'd been dog tired, though. Knackered. So when he got home, he'd started undressing in his hallway, before going up to bed. He had three hours to kip before the alarm was going to go off, and the last thing he wanted was a row with the missus about his hours again. So he'd left his clothes downstairs, his handgun on the belt. The sub-machinegun he took upstairs, of course. But the Glock stayed there in the hall.

He knew he shouldn't have brought it home, but shit, when the hours were this daft, what the fuck were you supposed to do? If he'd driven to the airport armoury last night to dump his guns before going home, he'd have had no time to sleep. All the lads took risks sometimes—it was the old rule: don't get found out.

Well, he would be found out this time. Some fucker had broken into his house, gone through the stuff in the hall, and his Glock had been nicked. Bloody gone, just like that. Today he'd been able to get away without it, saying he'd left it behind, and he had the H&K, so there was little enough to be said, but when he got home tonight, he'd have to have a good hunt, just in case. Maybe it had fallen down behind the umbrellas, or got kicked along the hall . . . Andy just prayed—Jesus, please don't let it be—yes, that either the thing hadn't been taken by some crook who was going to use it to hold up a bank or something, or that it hadn't been thrown away in the road outside his house.

He'd looked, of course, he'd looked everywhere, and just now all he could feel was a cold sweat breaking out at the mere thought that he'd be discovered at any moment. He had to get back home and make sure that the thing wasn't just lying there.

God, but any moment he could be called to be asked what the fuck his gun was doing in the hands of some drugged up shite who'd been holding a hostage or . . .

'Andy? Stop that. We've got a shout on. Some wanker with bombs or something. Get tooled up again.'

*   *   *

He had to stop thinking of his real name. Now he was Ramón, not Jean-Jacques. Ramón Escobar. The lightness in his belly was unbearable as he peered down through the window at Britain.

It was surprisingly green. He wasn't used to that. In Bogotà the city lay almost dead on the equator, although at that height it was hard to believe sometimes. The weather was not too hot. Not like Africa. The temperature in Colombia remained constant, and there was little in the way of seasonal variation. No summer and winter, just a slight change, a little cooler or a little warmer.

Like this, it was very green. You took off from Bogotà airport, and all you could see for miles around were greenhouses. The hothouses spread all over the plain, and even when the plane lifted and the ground fell away from that high plateau up in the mountains, the glass reflected the light all about the area. They said that Colombia's biggest legal export was cut flowers to America, and . . . *Ramón* could believe it. Easily.

Here, though, the plane was slowly descending through wisps of pale cloud, and beneath the greenness was . . . darker. Not so rich and blooming as the plant life of Bogotà. It looked harsher, as though the trees and shrubs were struggling more to survive, and it was easy to see why as the aircraft drew nearer to the ground. Here the greyness of concrete and tarmac was all about, but without the bright colours of jacaranda and bougainvillea to ease the sight. No, here, all was unrelenting, grey, miserable, and he felt the tears welling again to think that this place was his refuge.

His sanctuary in his exile. His new motherland.

* * *

The system was well worked out, and they swung into action as soon as the papers had been digested.

Paul walked casually away from the main hall as soon as he had checked the details in the print out and glanced up at the arrivals display. The plane was close, but not here yet. He had time.

Jeannie had seen the discussion, and now was play-acting as only she could. She looked up at the boards, and frowned at her watch, looking about her with a discontented expression, before wandering off in the direction of the women's toilets. Paul made his own way through a security barrier with a palmed card shown discreetly to the man at the gate, and into the Special Branch section. She was waiting for him.

'What's going on?'

He passed her the papers. 'Terrorist, they reckon. Bloke from Colombia. He's used this ID before—it was noted when the IRA Three were over there. It's fake. Why the hell he didn't get something new before taking off . . .'

'Perhaps no time?' She frowned as she

absorbed the description of the man.

'He was with FARC, the terrorists who control the country out towards Venezuela,' Paul said. He shivered. This was the kind of incident he had feared. 'They were trained by the IRA in new bombs and mortars. This Escobar was a cousin of one of the cartel leaders from Medellìn, and he escaped the crack down when his cousin was killed. He made it to Panama originally, then turned up back in Colombia with FARC. Now he's coming here.'

'Why?'

'Jesus! I don't know, all right?' he snapped. 'All we have to do is find him and watch, just like we always do. And when we see him, we go live on radio in case we have to call in the shooters.'

Jeannie nodded, and he saw a small smile of satisfaction on her face—she liked to needle him. There was a reasonably fresh brew of coffee in the jug. She poured, added a good slug of milk, and sipped it easily, walking from the room out to the main hall again, leaving him alone with his fears.

He should have been honest about his education, but when he was interviewed, he assumed that they'd never want him for active duties. He'd said he was good with languages, because that was what his mate said they wanted, but it never occurred to him that he'd be needed. God—the nearest he'd got to

270

languages was a smattering of Bantu and Ndebele when he took a gap year to study anthropology in Botswana.

Anyway, when he wrote out his CV, no one had seemed remotely interested. There'd been no time for checks. Perhaps someone would spot his lying later, when they went back through the CVs they'd collected in the last years since 9/11. Probably not, though. Human Resources had been reduced as they increased the Watchers—if you spend in one area you have to cut a budget elsewhere—and now there weren't the HR people to check all the new staff, let alone trawl through existing ones.

At his interview they were more keen on his post as a prefect at school. Responsible character, they'd said. No one had guessed he'd lied about that as well.

His eyes were drawn back to the sheet of paper, to the words that were highlighted: *Paul Jeffries to keep close. Spanish essential.*

Shit!

*　　　*　　　*

The H&K was soon made ready again. The mag slammed into the gun and smacked with the palm of his hand to seat it. He pulled the cocking lever back and let it drive forward, stripping the first round from the magazine and leaving the gun cocked and ready. He switched on the safety, keeping his finger well away from the trigger. In the last few years more police officers had been wounded because of negligent discharges than by criminals. He had enough on his plate without that, sod it.

Jack was waiting at the door. 'Shit of a day to leave the Glock behind, eh?'

'Fuck it!' Andy hissed. They both walked out together, their guns across their chests, fingers clear, and they turned their radios on as they entered the thronging main hall.

*   *   *

The man who called himself Ramón knew a fair amount about Bogotà, but only from reading. Not many people went to the city unless they had to. The bombs, the bullets, the murdering, the kidnapping and ransoming all dissuaded tourists, not only foreign ones. Locals were as unlikely to travel there. Anyone could be stopped and kidnapped, and a man like him, with a price on his head, would be best served keeping off the roads. Travel was very dangerous. Just like home. Except here the terrorists and guerillas were better armed than the police, whereas back home only the police and army had guns. And the President's friends.

Bogotà was beautiful. Ringed by the high, dark peaks, the place had an atmosphere all of its own. He had thought that, sitting in the

272

Parc de Periodistas, waiting for the man to arrive with the new passport. There was a smell of thick smog in the air, and he could see the coal smoke rising from several chimneys in the tower blocks nearby. A sulphurous odour that caught in his throat, and yet the buildings were typical Spanish colonial in so many areas of the city, especially the older parts where the emeralds were sold for so little. Spanish, American, there were so many influences. It was a lovely country.

His contact was a scrawny man, with a sallow, pock-marked complexion and a thatch of filthy brown hair. He spoke English only haltingly, and that suited Ramón. Neither wanted to know much about the other, and Ramón had been assured he was safe. He'd paid well for the advice.

Their business was soon completed, an envelope with much of Ramón's remaining cash, all in US dollars, was passed over, and in exchange a fake passport, driving licence, and some local identification cards. With these Ramón was safe. With these he could fly from the country and not be turned away at British immigration. It was too easy for asylum-seekers to be refused now, unless they had applied before leaving their homes, but he couldn't apply back home, and no one would help in Colombia. They had other things to worry about: terrorists and drug-dealers.

The jerk of the wheels hitting tarmac

brought him back to the present. In his bag in the hold there was the explosive material, and soon he would be in a position to light the touch-paper, he told himself.

*   *   *

Paul's first warning was the nod from immigration. There was no need for a buzzer or pager to call when a Watcher was present. Only if there was an immediate danger did they 'hit the tit' for the armed fuzz. Otherwise everything had to be managed silently, with a minimum of fuss to alert the bad guys that they were being followed.

At the carousel Paul stood back, watching his mark. Not tall, but well muscled, and a face that spoke of a warmer climate than Britain in November. Yes, he was the one, all right. There were plenty of Spaniard-types on the place, but this one definitely fitted the photo and profile best. Jeannie was down in the carousel hall, and they had a dummy bag for her to collect. She stood near the mark, and grabbed her bag as it came round.

Paul took a deep breath, shivering with expectation. Then he walked out through the customs tunnel, walking through the red channel and waiting with his own small luggage bag in case the target came this way. Jeannie would wait until he had left, then go through green no matter what.

The customs officer was a slim blonde girl, and she waited with Paul patiently until he had the signal from another officer. Then Paul hurried through the channel and out into the main hall.

*　　*　　*

Jack and Andy were waiting idly when the call came through.

'He's in the main hall now. Following him out.'

Andy beckoned with his head and wandered over to the main arrivals corridor. There was a family, then a couple of teens with backpacks, long fair hair straggling. A gap, a long gap. Andy felt his palms begin to sweat. He took his pistol hand away from the H&K and wiped it down his trousers, willing himself to look a little away from the corridor, but unable to obey. The bright fluorescent glow of the arrival tunnel transfixed him. He saw the tall figure appear.

*　　*　　*

Ramòn. Ramòn. Not Jean-Jacques Bressonard. He had to remember his new name until he could get his package delivered, but the officials on all sides petrified him. There was a young brunette watching him, and he forced himself to blink slowly, smiling through his exhaustion, looking away innocently and striding on determinedly, through the wide corridor, turning right at the end, passing through the crowds. He was safe.

There were two policemen in armour ahead of him, and he hardly glanced at them. He was thinking about his ancestors. They had fled from the terror in France, first arriving here in England, then making the long and dangerous journey to Africa. There they had thrived until the independence, until the new regime.

Over the centuries, England had remained their homeland. They owed their existence to the British who welcomed his Huguenot forebears. His grandfather volunteered and died in the trenches of the first war, his father nearly died in the Battle of Britain as a Hurricane pilot. Yes, Ramón was coming home.

In his own land he had ceased to exist. When his ID card was confiscated, he became a non-person. A man with no ID was nothing. He had no rights.

He smiled and nodded to the police, but then a chill entered his blood as he took in their faces: dead; cold, inhuman. Just like at home.

Walking more swiftly, he went right, avoiding them. Ahead of him was a beautiful woman, just like his lovely Miranda, and he felt a pang in his breast at the thought. He missed his family so much . . . but hopefully he could have them rescued too. They could come here to this cold, grey country.

For a moment he thought he could hear Miranda calling to him: 'Good morning!' just one instant before he saw the gun, realised it was flashing, felt the slugs hit his breast, and collapsed slowly, sinking to his knees even as the police emptied their H&Ks into him.

*   *   *

'Fuck, fuck, fuck!'

Andy shivered, his finger still tight on the trigger as he stood over the body.

'Cease firing! Cease firing! Cease firing!'

The terrorist was down, bullet wounds weeping all over his torso. An eye was punctured, and wept jelly, and Andy could only stare, too shocked even to feel sick yet. That would come later.

'Andy. ANDY! Get a fucking grip. Secure the place! Come on!'

'Why'd he do that? Why'd he fire?'

*   *   *

Paul had been hit twice that he knew of. He had been behind the target when he saw the man's body jerk and collapse, saw the bullets strike from the police guns, saw the body suddenly lifeless like a dummy, arms flailing as he was thrown to the side.

277

'No need for Spanish after all!' he said, almost giggling with reaction.

At his side a young girl was weeping, sprawled, a bloody mess on her back to show the exit wound. Near her a man was still and silent, an elderly woman was slumped by the wall, staring with surprise at a bloody hole in her belly, while her husband stood beside her with an expression of spaniel-like hurt and confusion. Paul gazed about him at them all, and tried to stand, but couldn't. All he could do was sit and watch as the police bellowed at the people in the area to get clear. Dazed, he looked up at the policeman with the sub-machinegun when he approached, and began to wonder what he might do. He'd just seen the man empty his magazine into a crowd.

'There's an ambulance on its way,' Jack said. He stood behind Andy. 'You all right?'

'I'm hit.'

'I can see that.'

Paul shook his head, tasted bile. 'Why did she say that? Why did she call to him and shoot him?'

Jack sighed and walked off. Andy frowned. 'Who did?'

'Jeannie,' Paul said. He choked a little on the phlegm that had materialised in his throat. 'My partner. Where is she?'

*   *   *

278

It was late when Andy returned to the gun room. He sat on the bench, exhausted. Jack walked in a few minutes later to unload his weapon.

'You all right?'

'I'm fine.'

'Unload, then. Come on, Andy! Unload.'

Andy stood and fumbled with the cocking lever, but there was nothing to do. His magazine was empty. Instead he pulled the mag free and stared at it dumbly.

Jack eyed him, then unloaded his own weapon. It was unfired. He set it in the safe, and as he did so, his foot kicked something under the bench. 'Shit, Andy—is that your gun? You didn't lock it in the safe, you prick!'

Andy jerked awake from his nightmare and gazed at Jack dumbly. Seeing the direction of his pointing finger, he reached down and took up the Glock in its holster. He hefted it in his hand, pulled it free. It had been fired. He could smell the powder in the barrel. And when he looked closer, the serial number on the side was one he knew all too well.

His hand began to tremble.

*   *   *

Paul took the advice from the ambulance driver, still shivering slightly as the needle went in and he watched the clear liquid pushed into his arm. The wounds were small: one

279

bullet had winged his shoulder, which was already as sore as hell, and a second had caught his rib, running around the outside of it, and ending up in his back after running around underneath his skin. The medic had offered to cut it loose, but he refused the offer.

'You'll need it taken out soon,' the medic said. He didn't bother to add that Paul would have to have the entire bullet's track opened and cleaned to remove all the bits of material and burned powder, or risk septicemia.

'Davie? Where is she?'

'Who? Jeannie? I told her to go home. She was in shock.'

Paul shivered. Davie looked at him sympathetically. 'Look, Paul, you need to rest, mate. Get on home.'

'She murdered the guy.'

'What?'

'She had a handgun. I saw her. She shouted something and opened fire. The cops started shooting as soon as she started. She started it, though. I saw her.'

'What did she shout? Spanish?'

'Lotjhani—in Ndebele it means "Hello".'

'Are you sure?'

The files in the bags were exhaustive. Details of murders, of officially sanctioned brutality. Paul shivered as he took in pictures of bodies in streets, strewn in fields, punctured with gunshots, or slashed with pangas, and he felt the sickness in his belly.

'Who is he?' Dave muttered.

'An asylum seeker. We killed an asylum seeker from Zimbabwe,' Paul spat. The pain was washing through him now as he stared at the sheet of paper, and he could feel a cold sweat run over his spine. Nausea roiled in his belly. 'And Jeannie murdered him.'

Perhaps, he wondered, the HR team hadn't only cocked up with *his* application?

*   *   *

The woman he had known as Jeannie climbed out of the car with the diplomatic plates, and walked in through the guarded doors into the High Commission as the car purred round to the parking space. The lift took her up, and soon she was seated, waiting for the debriefing, running the events through her mind once more.

It had been perfect. The theft of the policeman's firearm was a calculated risk, but when she had seen the changed rotas, it seemed a good bet. All the police took their guns home occasionally, even though it was officially disapproved of, and when a man had to travel far to his next shift, it made sense for him to keep his gun nearby. And the gamble paid off.

She had waited for the man this morning, and he had passed her the Glock at the airport entrance. The theft had gone without a hitch.

281

The fool was too exhausted to hear the two as they rifled his clothing and bags. After that all she had to do was wait until she saw Bressonard while the police man was present. Shoot, and run. They'd said that the police expected a terrorist, so they'd shoot as soon as they heard shots, and they'd been right. They always saw what they expected, or what they feared. No one would suspect her, a 'spook'.

So the enemy of the country was dead. He had been led carefully down a route pre-planned for him. A contact with FARC had agreed to provide obvious ID for him, and then they had known which aircraft he would take to Britain, and now he was dead. Well, now the world would see what a safe country Britain was for asylum-seekers. Like the Brasilian, a white farmer had been removed, and the police were guilty of his homicide. Either the machinegun or the pistol had killed him, and both were one officer's weapons.

The woman who had been called Jeannie removed her ID and placed it carefully before her on a glass-topped table. She wouldn't need these again. No. She was looking forward to returning to her own name. Her real one.

And returning to the glorious Zimbabwe sun, of course. Perhaps she could buy a small farm. Maybe even take Bressonard's?

Life was good.

InDex

Martin Edwards

(Being an extract from a draft index to *Celebrity Lawyer*, the autobiography of Jude Wykeham)

Wykeham, Jude

Affair
    With Esther Yallop
Autobiography
    Mysterious disappearance of
    Paid enormous sum to write
    Posthumous publication, anticipated
Guilt
    Presumed motive for suicide
Launch Party
    Meets Esther Yallop at
Police investigation of
    Errors in
    Fake suicide note, misled by
Publisher
    Shared with Esther Yallop
Puerto Banus,
    Purchase of holiday home at
    Weekends spent with Esther Yallop in
Queen's Counsel
    High earnings as

Rhetorical skills
    Seduction, persistent employment of when
    engaged in
Strangling
    Suspected of
Suicide
    Apparent

Yallop, Esther

Dress
    Expensive tastes in
    Provocative
Erotic poems
    Authorship of
    Lover, dedicated to
Husband, boredom with
Sarcasm, gift for
Strangulation of
    Pleasure taken in
    Remorse for, subsequent

Yallop, William

English degree, uselessness of
Indexer, part-time employment as
Manuscript
    Re-writing of
    Theft of
Novels, unpublished
Personality

285

Contributors

Carla Banks, who also writes as Danuta Reah grew up with stories. Her father, a Belarusian cavalry officer, kept his past alive by telling his children stories of his destroyed homeland. Her books are dark, with page-turning suspense. Her latest book, *The Forest of Souls* looks at the consequences of Nazi atrocities in Eastern Europe. Her next book, *Strangers*, set in the ex-pat community in Saudi Arabia, comes out in January 2007.

Robert Barnard had a distinguished career as an academic before he became a full-time writer. His first crime novel, *Death of an Old Goat*, was written while he was professor of English at the University of Tromso in Norway. The creator of several detectives, including Perry Trethowan and Charlie Peace, Barnard regards Agatha Christie as the ultimate crime writer and has published an appreciation of her work, *A Talent To Deceive*. Barnard was the winner of the 2003 CWA Cartier Diamond Dagger Award for a lifetime of achievement.

Tonino Benacquista has been, in turn, a museum night watchman, a train guard, a professional parasite on the Paris cocktail circuit, and one of the most successful authors of fiction, graphic novels, and film scripts in France today. Recent screenplays include *De battre mon coeur s'est arrêté* (The Beat My Heart Skipped) and *Sur mes lèvres* (Read My Lips), both directed by Jacques Audiard. His novel *Morsures de l'aube* (Love Bites) was adapted for the cinema by Antoine de Caunes. His novels have previously won the Trophee 813 and the Grand Prix des lectrices de Elle, and two are currently available in English from Bitter Lemon Press: *Holy Smoke* and *Someone Else*. His story here, *La Boîte noire*, taken from the collection *Tout l'ego*, was converted into a film by Richard Berry in 2005.

Natasha Cooper worked in publishing, then wrote historicals and relationship novels under another name, before finding her ideal home in crime fiction. Her current series character is Trish Maguire, a London barrister. When Natasha is not working on her latest novel, she writes feature articles and reviews for a variety of publications, including *The Times*, the *TLS*, and the *Toronto Globe & Mail*. She chaired the CWA in 2000.

Mat Coward's stories have been nominated for the Dagger and the Edgar, and published and broadcast in many countries. He writes the Don and Frank series of whodunit novels for *Five Star*. His other books include *Success And How To Avoid It*, and *Classic Radio Comedy*. Coward is gardening correspondent for the *Morning Star*.

Martin Edwards' Lake District Mysteries are *The Coffin Trail*—shortlisted for the Theakston's Crime Novel of the Year 2006—and *The Cipher Garden*. His seven novels about Harry Devlin include *All the Lonely People*, short-listed for the CWA John Creasey Memorial Dagger. The author of a stand-alone psychological thriller, *Take My Breath Away*, he also completed the late Bill Knox's last book, *The Lazarus Widow*. A well-known critic and commentator on crime fiction, he has contributed essays to various reference books, including *The Oxford Companion to Crime and Mystery Writing*.

Kate Ellis was born and raised in Liverpool and now lives in north Cheshire. Interested in history and archaeology, she is the author of ten crime novels, the latest of which is *The Marriage Hearse*. Her eighth novel, *The Plague Maiden* was nominated for the Theakston's Crime Novel of the Year in 2005 and she has twice been shortlisted for the CWA Short Story Dagger.

Paul A. Freeman was born in London. He is the author of *Rumours of Ophir*, a crime thriller set in Zimbabwe. Presently Paul Freeman works as a teacher in Saudi Arabia and writes a weekly short story for the *Saudi Gazette* newspaper. He is married with three children.

Edward D. Hoch is a past president of Mystery Writers of America and winner of its Edgar Award for best short story. He received MWA's Grand Master Award in 2001. Author of some 920 published stories, he has appeared in every issue of *Ellery Queen's Mystery Magazine* for the past 33 years. Hoch and his wife Patricia reside in Rochester, New York.

Michael Jecks writes the best-selling Templar series set in medieval Devon. Jecks was Chairman of the Crime Writers' Association 2004/2005, and was founder member of the Medieval Murderers touring group. He is keen to promote new writing, and judges competitions for the CWA. He lives in Dartmoor, where he walks his dogs, and occasionally terrifies audiences with his lack of ability as a Morris dancer.

Bill Kirton has been a university lecturer, actor, director, television presenter and RLF Writing Fellow. He's published two crime novels, *Material Evidence* and *Rough Justice,* and many short stories. His radio and stage plays have been produced in the UK, Australia, and the USA and he wrote a prize-winning verse translation of Molière's *Sganarelle.* Kirton is currently co-authoring a book on writing at university.

Five collections of **Peter Lovesey**'s short stories have been published, the latest *The Sedgemoor Strangler & Other Stories of Crime* in 2001. He has won several short story awards including the Ellery Queen Readers' Prize, the CWA Veuve Clicquot Award and the Mystery Writers of America Golden Jubilee Prize.

291

A short story is a rare departure for **Stuart Pawson**, who is more widely known as creator of the series of police procedurals featuring Detective Inspector Charlie Priest. He lives in Yorkshire and the local landscape often forms a backdrop to his work. Stuart has twice been shortlisted for the CWA Dagger in the Library and longlisted for the Theakston's Old Peculier award.

Christine Poulson had a career as an art historian before she turned to crime. She has written three novels set in Cambridge, featuring academic turned amateur detective, Cassandra James, the most recent being *Footfall*. She has also written widely on nineteenth century art and literature and is a research fellow in the Department of Nineteenth Century Studies at the University of Sheffield.

Zoë Sharp has worked as a freelance photojournalist in the automotive industry since 1988. She is also the author of five crime thrillers in the Charlotte 'Charlie' Fox series. The sixth title, *Second Shot*, is to be published shortly in the US by St Martin's Minotaur. Sharp is currently working on the first of a new series, to feature CSI Grace McColl.

Frank Tallis is a practicing clinical psychologist. He has written four novels: *Killing Time, Sensing Others* (Penguin), *Mortal Mischief,* and *Vienna Blood* (Random House). In 1999 he received a Writers' Award from the Arts Council of Great Britain, in 2000 he won the New London Writers' Award (London Arts Board), and in 2005 he was short listed for the CWA Ellis Peters Historical Dagger. He lives in London.

Yvonne Eve Walus is a mathematician and a writer. Her mystery novels are a cross between the modern and the cosy. In *Murder @ Work*, her second South African murder mystery, she explores the effect of political change on the white middle class.

Acknowledgements

The publisher would like to thank the following for their help and inspiration: Ann Cleeves, Isabelle Croissant, Zoe Lambert, Melanie Laurent, Gordana 'Goga' Matic, Snjezana Husic, Ana Makek, Morana Peric, Vera Juliusdottir, Mirjana 'Piki' Cibulka, Olga Šunyara, and Roman Simic. Thanks are also due to the tireless Comma crew: Maria Crossan, Jim Hinks and especially in this case Tom Spooner.